DAVID LUBAR  DUNK

Clarion Books • New York

For my dear friend and fellow writer Marilyn Singer,
who knows the value of a good laugh

Clarion Books
a Houghton Mifflin Company imprint
215 Park Avenue South, New York, NY 10003

Text copyright © 2002 by David Lubar

The text was set in 13-point Sabon.

www.houghtonmifflinbooks.com

Printed in the U.S.A.

Library of Congress Cataloging-in-Publication Data

Lubar, David.
Dunk / by David Lubar.
p. cm.
Summary: While hoping to work as the clown in an amusement park dunk tank on the New Jersey shore the summer before his junior year in high school, Chad faces his best friend's serious illness, hassles with police, and the girl that got away.
ISBN 0-618-19455-X
[1. Amusement parks—Fiction. 2. Clowns—Fiction. 3. Interpersonal relations—Fiction. 4. Sick—Fiction. 5. Beaches—Fiction. 6. New Jersey—Fiction.] I. Title.

PZ7.L96775 Du 2002
[Fic]—dc21   2001058428

QUM 10 9 8 7 6 5 4

HIS VOICE RIPPED THE AIR LIKE A CHAIN SAW. THE HARSH CRY sliced straight through my guts the first time I heard it. The sound cut deep, but the words cut deeper. He shredded any fool who wandered near the cage. He drove people wild. He drove them crazy. Best of all, he drove them to blow wads of cash for a chance to plunge his sorry butt into a tank of slimy water.

This was just about the coolest thing I'd ever seen. Which made it that much more amazing, since I lived in one of the coolest places on the planet and I'd seen some of the freakiest things man or nature had ever created.

I was on my way down the boardwalk to get a slice of pizza at Salvatore's. Today was the start of the tourist season. The crowds were thin because the ocean water was still chilly. That wouldn't last. In a few weeks the place would be mobbed. It would stay that way until the end of summer—wall-to-wall tourists frantically packing as much activity as possible into their vacation at the Jersey shore. I hoped someone special would also return. But if I thought about her too much right now, I knew I'd go crazy.

Thin crowds or not, a dozen people had gathered near the tank, watching, listening, laughing at the marks. That's what you call someone who's about to play a game—a mark. Or a vic, which is short for victim. I'd seen dunk tanks before, but I'd never paid much attention to them. Not until now.

The whole tank wasn't more than five feet wide and maybe eight feet high. The bottom half was filled with water, the top half was protected by iron bars. The protection was *definitely* necessary. A shelf on a hinge ran along the back wall. A metal target attached to a lever stuck out from the left side of the booth. The other end of the lever supported the shelf. Behind the target, a large sheet of canvas hung from a wire stretched between two poles. A wooden sign in front of the cage simply said:

DUNK THE BOZO
3 BALLS FOR $2

That pretty much explained the object of the game.

Ten feet in front of the cage, a guy with a change apron—a barker—sold balls to the players. This barker didn't have to do much barking—the game sold itself. I edged closer but stayed behind the crowd so I wouldn't attract the Bozo's attention. I shouldn't have worried. He wouldn't waste his breath on some kid who looked like he didn't have more than five bucks in his pocket. What would be the point in that? He sure wasn't there because he liked falling into a pool of bacteria soup. He was there to rake in the dollars.

"*Hey!*" the Bozo shouted at a guy near the front of the small crowd. "Where'd you get that wig? You scalp it off a poodle?"

The crowd laughed and the guy's face turned the color of a bad sunburn. His right hand jerked up toward his head, as if he wanted to adjust the fake hair that was plastered there.

"Yeah, you," the Bozo shouted, pointing straight at the guy, turning himself into a nightmare version of an Uncle Sam poster. "What's the matter? Did you get glue in your ears when you pasted on that wig?"

The mark yanked his wallet from his pocket and whipped out a couple bucks. The barker traded the money for three baseballs he'd grabbed from a plastic five-gallon bucket at his feet. He did all this with one hand while holding a half-eaten hot dog in the other. I noticed mustard and ketchup smeared on the change apron tied over his belt. Crumbs littered the front of his shirt and dangled from the shaggy fringe of his mustache, making me think of snowflakes on a pine branch.

"Imagine that," the Bozo said, his voice growing less harsh as he spoke to the crowd. It was almost like he was sharing a secret with us. "Somewhere there's a poor dog running around with a bare butt so this guy can have a curly head. Woof, woof."

"Oof," the mark grunted as he threw the first ball.

Thwunk! The ball smacked the large sheet of canvas, missing the target by at least a foot. The back of the mark's neck grew even redder.

"Hhhhhaaaaawwwwhhhoooooheeeeeeeyyaaaa!" The Bozo leaned close to the microphone that hung from the top of the cage and let loose with a screaming laugh, another chain saw through my guts. "If that's your best throw, you'd better just mail the other balls to me. Anybody got a stamp?" His grin was amplified by a huge red smile. He wore a clown's face—white forehead and cheeks, black stars around the eyes, red painted nose. Like most clowns, he was scary as hell.

Thwunk! Ball two. Nothing but canvas. It sounded like a pro wrestler getting body slammed.

"If I had your arm, I'd trade it for a leg," the Bozo screamed. "Hhhhhaaaaawwwwhhhhooooheeeeeeyyaaaa!"

Above us, a flock of circling sea gulls squawked in agreement.

The mark, his face as red as the Bozo's nose, hurled the last ball so hard he nearly fell over. I could feel my own shoulder muscles burning in sympathy.

Thaaaaawunnnk! I jumped back as the baseball smacked the canvas. A couple people chuckled, but most of the crowd murmured sounds of sympathy. They were beginning to root for this clumsy David to luck out and drown Goliath.

I braced for the laugh, but the Bozo surprised me. "Aw, shucks," he said, quietly. "That was really close. I was sure you had me that time." He looked down for a moment, as if he'd lost interest in the guy. Then, before the mark was even two steps away, the Bozo snapped his head back up and shouted, "Looooooooserrrrrrrrrrrrrrrrrrrrrrr!"

The word stretched out like a cheap motorcycle engine stuck in first gear.

I couldn't believe it. The mark spun back so fast, I thought his wig would fly off. His hand was already digging for his wallet. He wasn't a person anymore—he was a puppet. The Bozo had control.

The guy missed again with all three balls. Before the last ball had even stopped rolling, he'd bought another round. This time his third throw nicked the edge of the target, but not hard enough to trip the lever under the Bozo's seat. The crowd let out a sigh of disappointment.

The poor vic went through twelve dollars before he finally nailed the target, sending the Bozo plunging into the water. It caught me by surprise. He'd missed so many times, I figured he'd never score.

"So there," the mark said as he strutted away, smirking. Amazing—he'd just blown more money than a lot of people make in an hour, and he was leaving empty-handed. No prize of any kind. But he still acted like a winner.

In less than a blink, the Bozo lifted the platform, locked it in place, and scampered back to his seat. He reminded me of a seal slithering out of a pool. As he flicked his head to the side, throwing a shower of water from his hair, I realized he'd already picked his next vic.

"Hey, lady," he said, staring at a woman who was laughing at him. "I may be wet, but you're funny looking. And tomorrow, guess what? I'll be dry."

He paused for an instant as the crowd grew quiet, then added, "Yeah, I'll be dry, and you'll still be funny looking. Haaaaaaahhooeeee!"

Thwunk.

Thwunk.

Thwunk.

She did better than the guy. It only took her eight bucks to get satisfaction and revenge. She walked away with a dark smile.

Not me.

My shoes might as well have been nailed to the boardwalk. I forgot all about pizza. Even the drifting scent of candy from the NutShack over to my left didn't lure me away. An hour passed. Maybe two. I watched and listened, unable to tear myself from the performance of this outrageous clown.

For the first time in my life, I knew something for dead certain. Some way, somehow, I had to have a turn. Not throwing balls at the target. I wasn't going to waste money trying to dunk the Bozo. No, I wanted to be on the other side. I wanted to make the marks dance like puppets on a string. I wanted to shout and scream at the world from the safety of a cage.

I wanted to be the Bozo.

2

WHEN I FINALLY LEFT TO GET THAT SLICE OF PIZZA, A wonderful scene filled my mind. I imagined the Bozo sitting in the back of Ms. Hargrove's class. She'd been my history teacher last year. All she ever said to me was, "You'll never get anywhere in this world, Chad Turner." Just because of what happened the first day. Things were fine until I noticed that every third or fourth sentence, she'd nod her head and say, "That's the truth." I couldn't help trying to guess when those words would pop out next. I got pretty good at it after a while. Then I started keeping count. I swear I was hypnotized. *Blah blah, blabitty blah. That's the truth. Blah blah, babble, blah. That's the truth. Blah blah. . . .* Her words all became sound without meaning.

I was so busy listening to how she talked, and watching this little flap of skin under her chin wiggle with each head nod, that I forgot to pay any attention to what she was talking about. Or who she was talking to. Then, too late, I realized she was talking to me.

"You. I just asked you a question."

I tried to sort back through her words and figure out what she'd asked. I thought I remembered her saying something about Columbus. "Fourteen ninety-two?" I guessed.

She glared at me. I looked past her to the board. No clues there.

"Well?" Ms. Hargrove turned up the temperature on the glare.

I knew what I wanted to say. *Don't ask me. You're the one who was alive back then.* But I wasn't in the mood for a trip to the office. I'd practically lived there the year before. "I don't know. . . ." I admitted.

She lowered her head and unleashed the full power of the lasers that lurked beneath her eyebrows. "Of course you don't know. It's obvious you weren't even paying attention. That's the truth. I can't understand why they let troublemakers like you into my class. You'll never amount to anything. That's the truth."

From then on, she seemed angry every time she looked in my direction. *That's definitely the truth.* She never gave me a break. I'd bet the Bozo wouldn't give her a break, either. I could just see her face when he let loose.

Hey, you! Why don't you try smiling for a change? Afraid your teeth will fall out?

Thawunk. She'd throw the chalk. Not even close. *Thawunk.* The eraser. Missed by a mile, leaving a patch of chalk dust on the wall. The Bozo would shoot back another stunning line. *Thawunk.* Flying stapler. Another miss. As the scene played out in my mind, Ms. Hargrove emptied her desk of every throwable object, then finished up by yanking out her false teeth and hurling them at the Bozo. They shattered with a satisfying crash against the wall. Molars went flying. Canines bounced on the floor like Tic Tacs.

I laughed out loud at the image.

But school was done, and Ms. Hargrove was nothing

more than an unpleasant memory. I'd never be in her class again. I'd never be a tenth grader again, trapped in a room with any of those other teachers who thought I was a loser. I had the whole summer ahead of me. And I was in the perfect place for enjoying myself. Between the beach and the boardwalk, this was heaven on earth. And right now I was headed for a tasty part of that heaven.

Halfway to Salvatore's, I heard another amazing sound. Actually, it was three sounds: *ploop* . . . . . . *BAWAP!* . . . *humph* . . . . *ploop* . . . . . . *BAWAP!* . . . . *humph* . . .

I went to the beach side of the boardwalk and leaned over the railing. Sure enough, there was my buddy Jason, working out by himself at a volleyball court. He backed away from the net and hit the ball, *ploop,* sending it up about fifteen feet. As it fell, he moved into position, then leaped up for a monster spike. *BAWAP!* Microseconds later, the ball plowed into the sand with the force of a rocket. *Humph.*

In one smooth motion Jason slipped under the net, chased after the ball, and scooped it up. He reminded me of a surfer or a cartoon Tarzan sliding through the jungle. That's the funny thing about Jason. If you took a quick glance at him, you'd think *California beach bum,* since he's big and strong with bright blond hair that looks like it's been baking in the sun all his life. No way. He's a city kid. He moved here from New York three years ago.

"Hey," I called. "Want to get a slice?"

"Later," Jason called back. He held up the ball. "Want to play?"

"No, thanks." There'd be plenty of time for volleyball. Besides, it wasn't exactly my best sport. I'd been on the wrong end of Jason's spikes too often. Even when he took it easy, the ball shot at me with enough force to do damage. Once, just for fun, he played me with his right hand behind his back. He still kicked my butt. It was like playing against a cannon.

Three girls in halter tops and shorts walked near the railing and glanced down at the beach. They actually stopped and whispered to each other for a moment when they caught sight of Jason. I thought about saying hi, but they didn't notice me.

"Fan club," I said after they'd moved on.

Jason shrugged. He never seemed to let it go to his head.

"See you tonight?" I asked.

"Sure. Around seven?" He jogged to the pole on the far side of the net and grabbed a bottle of water.

"Yeah. Meet me at my place."

Jason nodded, then took a big gulp from the bottle. Too big. He coughed, spraying water across the sand.

"Hey, better lay off the cigarettes," I told him. That was a joke, since Jason was a total health nut. I think he had about minus seven percent body fat.

He was still coughing, but not as violently. "You okay?" I asked.

He nodded, so I headed off. I went to Salvatore's and bought two slices to go, eating them as I walked back to my place. My pleasure lasted until I got inside. The moment I saw Mom's face, I knew she was excited about something. Unfortunately, her idea of good news was usually a world apart from mine.

3

"GUESS WHAT? I FOUND A NEW TENANT," MOM SAID BEFORE I even had a chance to close the door.

"Wonderful." I tried to say it without groaning too much. We owned the whole house, but Mom rented out the second floor. Our living room and kitchen were pretty much one open space, with just a counter in between. Aside from that, we had a bathroom and a tiny bedroom. Mom got the bedroom. I slept on the foldout couch. I'm not complaining. I've seen too many people sleeping on the streets to ever bitch about any bed that had a roof over it. I'm just saying the place was about as small as a home could be and still be eligible for an address. When Mom—actually, Mom and Dad—had bought the place, they'd figured they'd live here for a while and then rent the house out. Work hard, buy more houses. The whole deal. Things hadn't turned out that way.

The apartment upstairs had the same layout, with a separate entrance. That was good, because I'd hate having a stranger walking through the house all the time. It's bad enough that someone would be living overhead. As I thought about the inevitable footsteps, I glanced up at the ceiling.

"He's not here right now. He's moving in later today," Mom said.

"I'm more interested in when he's moving out." The old tenant had left over a month ago, and I'd really hoped the place would stay empty for the summer.

"He's a very nice man," Mom said. "He came here last night while you were out. He's going to be teaching at the community college this fall."

Fall was a long way off. "Did you get a deposit?" I asked. Mom was so busy with work and her classes that she sometimes forgot stuff like that.

"He just started a summer job. He told me he'd have the money in a couple days."

"Oh, that's great. Listen, if he doesn't pay up by the end of the week, he's out of here." I couldn't believe she'd trust a stranger.

"That's not your decision," Mom said. She opened the fridge and grabbed a takeout bag from the diner.

"How'd he hear about it?" I asked. We hadn't put a sign in the window. That was an invitation for trouble. Mom spread the word to folks she knew.

"Doc over at the arcade gave him my name. If Doc says he's okay, I'm sure he'll be fine." She pulled a sandwich from the bag. "Tuna. Want half?"

"No, thanks." I gave up. There was no point in arguing. She'd already rented the place. Obviously, I wasn't going to win that battle. But a more important battle was waiting.

"We can use the extra money," Mom said as she sat down at the table.

No news flash there. We always needed money. The problem was, we couldn't even get that good a rental rate. We were three and a half blocks from the beach. The places right next to the boardwalk could charge a lot more. And you made the most money renting by the day or the week. But Mom wanted a long-term tenant. She'd had enough change in her life. So had I.

"Things are pretty tight right now," Mom added.

Talk about a perfect chance. "I saw a sign at the bookstore. They have a job opening. Full-time for the whole summer. Mr. Salazar over at the taco stand needs someone, too. He said he'd train me. There are openings all over the place." My fists clenched as I waited for an answer.

Mom shook her head. "You know how I feel about that."

Yeah, I knew how she felt about that. I fought the urge to kick the couch. "I've heard it a million times. You grew up so poor you couldn't even afford a dirt floor. You started working at the age of three. Or was it two? I forget." Why did she think her childhood had anything to do with my life? That was ancient history.

"Thirteen," Mom said. "It's nothing to joke about."

"But everyone has a job. Jason, Mike, Ellie." Jason worked almost every day after school, then knocked off in the summer so he could play volleyball. Mike worked summers for a guy who owned five game booths near the center of the boardwalk. And Ellie, who'd just graduated, had a summer job as a lifeguard.

"You'll be working your whole life once you get out of school," Mom said. "I want you to enjoy yourself while you can. Maybe next summer you can get a job."

"But—"

Mom took a step closer. "Look at me, Chad. I'm thirty-two, and I could probably pass for forty. That's what hard work will do to you."

And having a kid when you're seventeen, I thought. The guilt wrapped around the anger tight enough to smother it. I felt I'd drown if I didn't break the tension. "Hey, looking older wouldn't be so bad," I said. "If I could pass for twenty-one, I could buy beer."

Mom shook her head and smiled. I felt both of us relax. Then she had to say it. "You're so clever. You got your dad's way of talking."

"I've got *nothing* of him in me," I said, smacking the table hard enough to make my flesh sting. Why the hell did she have to mention that loser?

Mom balled up the remains of her sandwich in the bag and tossed it into the kitchen garbage, then started cleaning the counter, even though it was already clean.

I turned on the television and watched some idiot explain how easy it was to get rich if you followed his simple formula. Beyond the noise and chatter of the infomercial, a silence hung in the room. I wished she had a clue how I felt. I wasn't asking to spend sixteen hours a day in a factory. I was asking for permission to have a lousy summer job. Something to help keep me busy. Something to help keep me from screwing up.

4

WHEN THE INFOMERCIAL ENDED, I GLANCED OVER AT MOM, who was standing by the table watching me. She shifted her eyes toward the floor. "Things will be better soon. . . ."

"Yeah, it'll be okay," I told her. Though I knew things would be a lot better if she'd just let me help. Right now, Mom had a job as a waitress at the Leaping Dolphin Restaurant, which, despite the name, was really just a huge diner. She was taking classes at night to learn how to be a legal secretary, so she was only able to work the breakfast and lunch shifts.

Dad was two or three years behind on his support checks, and about as likely to catch up as I was to grow a third eye in the middle of my forehead. Not that we needed his help. The last time we'd heard from him, right before Christmas, he'd actually tried to borrow money from Mom.

So, as my friend Corey would say, we had a cash-flow problem. That's why we rented half of our house to strangers.

I guess it didn't matter about the apartment. I wasn't planning to spend much time indoors. Maybe the new tenant would be okay, if Doc had sent him. Doc owned the best arcade on the boardwalk. He looked like the world's largest gnome. He yelled a lot, but when he was in a good mood he let me play games for free. He paid me to run errands, too.

Since Mom wouldn't allow me to get a regular job, I picked up money running errands, like if a guy needed something and couldn't leave his shop, I'd go get it for him. They'd send me to the post office or ask me to pick up parts from the hardware store. I guess I owed the whole thing to Doc. One day a couple years ago, he'd asked me to grab a sandwich for him. When I got back, he'd told me to keep the change. It didn't take me long to figure out that there were plenty of other people willing to pay for five or ten minutes of my time.

It was okay with Mom if I ran odd jobs. I suppose she figured that wouldn't destroy my childhood. She acted like it wasn't real work, which was fine with me. When she mentioned it at all, she called it *doing favors*. There was just one problem—it wasn't steady. I might run my tail off one day and do nothing the next. I'd rather have a real job.

But it didn't matter what I wanted. Mom had said no. She pretty much let me do anything else I wanted, but she was flat-out unmovable when it came to this. I was paying for *her* bad experiences. It looked like I'd have to stick with the odd jobs for another year. There was no way I could stand being this close to the boardwalk all summer without any money. I'd go crazy. The whole place—food, games, rides, and all—was designed to make you spend. But I was careful where I spent my money. I knew enough to avoid the skill games. Most of them were a lot harder to win than they looked.

Take the basketball games. A real hoop is almost wide

enough to fit two balls at once. It looks small because it's high up. The hoops at the boardwalk were just big enough for one ball to squeeze through. And the balls had so much air in them that they bounced like a five-year-old on a chocolate overdose. You had to be pretty lucky to score.

Of course, some of the games were easy to win. That was on purpose, too. Nothing happened by chance around here—especially not at the games of chance. The trick was that an easy game meant a small prize. If you looked up "small prize" in the dictionary, I'd bet the definition would be "worthless crap." To get anything better, you had to trade up. It's amazing how quickly people lose their basic math skills when they've got their eyes locked on a giant stuffed Scooby-Doo.

Nope—I didn't drop much money playing the skill games. But I loved the rides. Especially the roller coasters. The more extreme, the better. They had a bargain session during the morning—maybe because it was hard to convince people to go upside down right after breakfast.

I also liked the video games. And I was hooked big-time on the soft ice cream. Especially chocolate peanut-butter twist. It was wonderful. I could feel my arteries clog up with each bite. Jason told me I'd need a new heart by the time I was twenty. I told him I'd borrow his.

But I didn't blow much money. I was saving up for after graduation. Jason had big plans to head for California. He was always talking about it, and I'd sort of played along, though I really wasn't sure what I wanted to do. All I knew was, whatever I did, it would help to have some cash.

I checked the clock. It was a little after three. I decided to hang out until Mom left for her classes. I didn't really do stuff with her. We each did our own thing. But between the restaurant and her school, I hardly saw her, so I liked to hang out when she was home, even if we ended up arguing sometimes.

At four thirty Mom headed out. And I headed into trouble.

5

IF YOU LAY OUT A COUPLE MILES OF GREAT FOOD AND FREE entertainment along a beautiful stretch of beach, you're going to attract more than just horseflies, sea gulls, and friendly tourists. Some dangerous lowlife can haunt the boardwalk. Mixed in with the vacation crowd was a scattering of thugs, muggers, dealers, and drunks. I knew enough to stay out of their way.

I especially avoided the dealers. And not just for fear of getting busted. Every time I went past some guy working his territory, I expected a spray of bullets to come flying through the air. Maybe I was overreacting. It had been nearly a year since a dealer had been shot, and that hadn't even happened on the boardwalk. He'd been killed over in the bad part of Abbot Drive, where a lot of the dealers lived. But I can't always control my imagination.

While I managed to keep clear of the full-time criminals, some of the amateurs were harder to avoid. I ran into one of them less than a block down the boardwalk.

"Hey, Chad. Whuz up?" Anthony Glover strutted out of the Royal Cabana Gift Shop and joined me as I wandered along near the railing. The Cabana was one of those shops that sold tourist stuff like knockoff T-shirts and beach mats. They had watches that said *Gucci* or *Rolex* on them even though it was obvious they'd come straight here from some pirate factory in China. You could get any designer label you wanted, as long as you didn't care if it was fake. Anthony was carrying something in his left hand, holding it low, next to his stomach. Sunglasses. I could see the price tag dangling from the hinge. I could also see an Oakley logo on the frame. A tingle rippled through me, brought to life by the thrill of free stuff, but I fought it off. This wasn't cool, and I didn't want any part of it.

I kept walking, but nodded so Anthony wouldn't think I was ignoring him. There was no point making enemies. He was a year ahead of me, but we'd been in the same wood-shop class, so I'd probably be stuck with him again.

Anthony glanced over his shoulder toward the Royal Cabana. He had the sort of face that mothers trusted. And he had the sort of smile girls loved. He also had the sort of heart you'd find in a snake, or a stone. Back when I was a freshman, we'd hung out a bit, until I'd figured out how slimy he really was. By then I'd already gotten into a bunch of trouble.

"Just act natural. Okay? Nobody saw me." He matched my stride, like we were the two best buddies in the world.

"I'm in a hurry," I said. I didn't feel like acting any particular way for his sake. I could still remember the time he'd trashed my bicycle. He'd sworn it was an accident, but I knew better. Anthony liked to ruin things.

"Look," he whispered, "just pretend we're together. No sweat."

"Stop!" A middle-aged man raced out of the Royal Cabana. "Thieves!" he shouted, pointing right at us.

Thieves? No. There was just one thief. I had nothing to do with this. I didn't even want any sunglasses.

The man yelled again.

"Catch you later, Chad." Anthony vaulted over the railing. I heard the dull thud of his sneakers smacking the sand six feet below, then the shuffling sound of him taking off.

I was jerked back as someone grabbed my wrist. "Hey, let go!"

"Thief," the man said, yanking on my arm. "Lousy thief."

"I didn't steal anything." I searched the gathering crowd for a friendly face. No luck. Everyone stared back with the half-guilty, sure-glad-it's-not-me smirk people get when they've just seen bad luck fall on a stranger. Except for one person. This joker in black jeans and a black turtleneck, sitting on the bench I'd just walked past, stared at me like he was watching television.

The man from the shop kept shouting at me. He'd switched into another language.

"Look," I said, "I didn't take anything." I patted my pockets with my free hand, then glanced back toward the guy on the bench. "You saw it, didn't you? I was here the whole time."

The guy didn't say anything. But somebody else did. "What's the problem here?"

Oh, crap. This was getting worse and worse. I hated hearing those words, especially when they were attached to a pair of cops. Cops didn't like me. Not just back when I'd hung out with Anthony. Even before then. Even after, I guess. Other words ran through my head. *You're so much like your dad.*

The man was still screaming. He'd let go of my arm, but I could feel where his fingers had dug into my wrist. I jammed my hands into my pockets to hide the shaking. Then I pulled them out because I was afraid the cops would think I was hiding something else. My whole body felt like it was buzzing. I struggled to look innocent, and wondered whether I should rat out Anthony. I didn't want to do that unless I had no other choice.

The man from the shop switched back into English long enough to tell the cops I was a thief who deserved to be whipped and thrown in jail.

The taller of the cops—Officer Manetti, according to his name tag—scanned the crowd and said, "Anybody see what happened?"

Suddenly, nobody was interested in us. They all slipped away. Except for the guy on the bench. "He saw it," I said. "I didn't do anything. I was just walking along. Ask him."

"You see it?" the cop called to the guy.

The guy shrugged.

The other cop, Officer Costas, glared at me. I could feel his gaze drilling through me, like he knew every detail of every bad thing I'd ever done. *Just* the bad things. He had the sort of eyes that couldn't see any of the good stuff.

"I'm not going to forget your face," he said.

It took a second for that to sink in. He was saying he'd be watching for me. But it also sounded like he was letting me go. I waited, afraid to do anything that might make him change his mind.

"You stay out of that shop," Officer Manetti said. "And you stay out of trouble. Okay?"

I nodded, not trusting my voice right now.

He turned to the man from the shop and pulled out a pad. "Can you describe the person who robbed you?"

"Him," the guy shouted, pointing at me. "He robbed me. Sunglasses. Designer label. All day they steal. I try to make an honest living. But they steal."

"No," Officer Costas said. "Tell us about the one who took the sunglasses. Understand?" I got the feeling he didn't like the man from the shop any more than he liked me. Maybe Officer Costas didn't like much of anything. Or anybody. Some people were born that way.

I moved a step away. They didn't seem to care. I took another step. I halfway expected Officer Costas to draw his gun and shout, *"Freeze!"* Maybe even fire a couple warning shots through my knees. But they were done with me.

I wasn't in any mood to hang out on the boardwalk. I wanted to get back home. As I walked past the jerk on the bench, I said, "Thanks for all the help."

"You're quite welcome." His expression didn't change.

I muttered several words comparing him to various body parts. I didn't care if he heard me.

I headed north to Fifteenth Street. Every block, there's a zigzag ramp and a set of steps that go down to the sidewalk. As I walked along the ramp, I caught sight of the guy from the bench about ten feet behind me. I guess he didn't appreciate my comments.

I could run. But the guy looked like he was in shape. He wasn't old. He wasn't a college student, either. Maybe ten or fifteen years past that. Thin. The kind of thin that comes from skipping meals. Hair a bit too long for someone his age, and damp like he'd just gotten out of the shower. Taller than me but shorter than Jason. I wasn't ready to find out which of us was faster.

He probably wasn't even following me. My house was across the street and around the corner on Sea Crest Avenue three blocks up. I crossed over.

The guy crossed, too. I noticed he walked kind of funny, dragging one foot a bit. Nothing real obvious, but just enough so the sound of his footsteps wasn't even. As I walked, I scanned the trash cans for anything I could use as a weapon. Nothing. Not even a broken broomstick.

When I turned at Sea Crest, he was still following me.

My house was only half a block away. If I sprinted, I figured I'd get enough of a head start to reach the front door before him. I slipped one hand in my pocket and touched my key.

I crossed the street again, moving to the side opposite where I lived, just to see for sure if he was following me. If he came over, I'd spin and make a dash for the house. He wouldn't expect that.

He stayed on his side. Man, the next breath I took was the deepest one of the afternoon. I slowed down, figuring I'd wait until after he walked out of sight before I crossed back and went inside.

Things didn't work out that way.

He stopped in front of my house.

It wasn't until he'd climbed halfway up the side steps that the obvious explanation smacked me in the face. "Wonderful. Just wonderful," I said as I watched him unlock the upstairs door.

The freak was our new tenant.

6

I KNEW EXACTLY WHERE HE WAS. EVERY TIME HE MOVED, I heard his footsteps. When he sat on the couch, the floorboards groaned over our own couch. For a while he stood by the front window. Then he walked to his refrigerator. I could even hear the thud of the fridge door closing.

I wanted to go upstairs and let him know what I thought of him. What kind of jerk doesn't stick up for someone who's in trouble? He could have told the cops I was innocent. But he'd just sat there. I flipped on the television, cranked the volume loud enough to annoy anybody living over my head, and tried to think about other things.

The knock on the door startled me. I looked at the clock over the sink. It was a couple minutes after seven.

"All set?" Jason asked when I opened the door.

"Yeah. Sure. Let's go." I locked up and followed him out to the sidewalk. This year there was something else besides the usual rides and games and food pulling me toward the boardwalk. Someone else.

"First night," Jason said.

"First of many," I said. Whatever problems might be living over my head, I wasn't going to let them spoil the night. Jason and I had a tradition. We would walk all the way to the far end of the boardwalk without spending a dime, then do any stuff that cost money on the way back. It helped stretch out our cash.

Usually we'd hook up with our other friends along the way. Jason and I lived at the north end of the boardwalk. But everyone hung out closer to the center, near Panic Pier.

We came down Fifteenth Street and went up the ramp. It would be dark in an hour or two. That was one of the best times on the boardwalk. A million flashing lights and a thousand blasting speakers filled the air with so much sound and color, you could almost swim in it.

"That's one place I won't be going," I said when we walked past the Royal Cabana Gift Shop. My stomach tightened as the memories played themselves back.

"Why not?"

I told Jason what happened.

"No big deal," he said. "It's not like you've never been kicked out of a shop before."

"Not in a while," I said.

"Besides, all the stuff he sells is total crap." He walked over to one of the shirts hanging above the entrance. Like many of the stores on the boardwalk, this one was open all along the front. "Cheap. Really cheap," he said, rubbing the cloth between his thumb and fingers. He glanced at the label. "Ten percent cotton. Ninety percent recycled toilet paper. Hand wash, then flush repeatedly."

There was a part of me that was dying to give the owner a real reason to call the cops. But there was no way I wanted to spend the first night of summer vacation locked up. I slipped toward the railing, far enough away so he wouldn't notice me. At the moment he had a much closer target for his anger. He glared at Jason from behind the register. "You! Stop touching!"

Instead of leaving, Jason strolled into the store. He went to the side wall and tapped a shirt that showed Mickey Mouse removing Donald Duck's head with an ax. "Hey, shouldn't there be like a trademark or a copyright or something?" Jason asked. "I don't think Disney gave anyone permission to show Mickey being so aggressive with an ax. And what about this one?" He tapped another rather nasty shirt. "I'm sure Charlie Brown wouldn't ever do that to Lucy."

"Go. Leave. Get out!" the man yelled. He sprang from his stool and hurried around the counter.

"Oh, my word," Jason said. He covered his eyes with one hand and pointed toward a rack of sweatshirts with the other. "Garfield would never be so evil."

"Go!" The man shouted, waving his arm toward the front of the shop. "I don't want your business!"

"Yes, sir," Jason said. "Have a nice day." He strolled back over to me. "Yeah. It's definitely junk. I think you could live to be a hundred and never need to go in there."

"That's not the point. The guy thinks I'm a thief. So do the cops." Just the mention of that made my face feel hot.

"Are you a thief?" Jason asked.

"No." A couple times, maybe. Little things. But not in the last few years. I remembered how Dad would bring stuff home. Weird junk, like a whole case of light bulbs, or a dozen red two-piece bathing suits. *Fell off the back of a truck,* he'd tell Mom. She'd get upset. Then he'd go off. I guess to sell it somewhere, because I'd usually see an empty whisky bottle in the garbage the next morning. "I'm not a thief," I said.

"Then why do you care what he thinks?"

"I don't know. I just care." I couldn't explain it. Jason didn't seem to worry what anybody thought. A thousand people could be lined up accusing him of something, and it would just roll off his back. But in reality, nobody ever accused him of anything. He never got in trouble. It was the one thing Jason and Anthony had in common. Though with Jason, at least, there was no deception. He really was what he seemed to be. He didn't have to work at it, either. People just naturally liked him. Jason probably could have said anything he wanted to Ms. Hargrove in history and she'd have patted him on the head and asked him to run for class president.

"*He's* the thief," Jason said, pointing back at the guy in the shop. "He sells cheap crap for a high price. I'll bet he cheats on his taxes, too."

"Come on. Let's just get away from here." I headed down the boardwalk.

"And Anthony's a jerk," Jason added as he caught up with me. "He's going to end up shot dead or in jail."

"Or shot dead in jail," I said.

Jason nodded.

We walked past the first pier, Sea Squall Mall. There were five piers on the boardwalk. Three were huge, with lots of rides—Wild Willy's, Panic Pier, and Thrillville. The smaller piers weren't very interesting. One was a public area with benches, but no rides or anything. The other—the one we were passing—just had stores on it.

Neither of us wanted to shop, so we moved on to Wild Willy's Pier, home of two awesome coasters and a half dozen other extreme rides that turned you upside down and inside out. "Hey," I said, remembering the incredible performance I'd stumbled across that afternoon, "you have to check this out. The guy's amazing." I wove my way around the games, leading Jason past the simulator ride and the NutShack. I headed for the right side of the wide entrance to the pier.

"Where are we going?" he asked.

"You'll see. This guy's totally unbelievable. Just don't get too close. He'll rip you right in half, chew you up, and spit you out before you even know what happened."

"That sounds like fun."

I rushed ahead. I didn't want to stay for long—I had somewhere else to go to. But I wanted Jason to see and hear the stunning performance I'd witnessed that afternoon.

"Hey, ugly," the Bozo called.

Jason caught up with me.

"Yeah, you, ugly," the guy in the tank said. "You're real ugly. You know that? They should call you Mr. Ugly." He looked toward the left side of the crowd, but didn't bother pointing at anyone in particular.

"What's the big deal?" Jason asked.

"Shoot. That's not him," I said. This Bozo was a lot heavier than the other guy. He wore pretty much the same clown makeup, but on him it just looked like someone who'd made a last-minute decision to go to a Halloween party. He wasn't creepy or spooky or much of anything. Just kind of pathetic.

Nobody took the bait. "Aren't you fat," the Bozo said, turning toward another part of the crowd. "You are so fat. They should call you Mr. Fat."

"This rots," Jason said. "The average three-year-old is sharper than that joker. Let's go."

"Yeah. *I* could do better. A lot better."

I stepped away. Behind me, I heard the Bozo say, "Aren't you stupid. They should call you Mr. Stupid."

Jason tapped my shoulder and nodded toward the barker running the game. He was the same guy from before, and he still held a part-eaten hot dog. I hoped it was a different one. "Yeah, I'll bet you could do better. Why don't you ask him to try you out?"

"Not now," I said. "He's busy."

There must have been something in my voice. Jason stared at me for a second, then said, "Good grief, you sound like you'd really want a chance to be a Bozo. Please tell me I'm wrong." Sometimes he had this spooky way of knowing what was on my mind.

I shrugged. "It looks like fun." I could imagine the Bozo tearing into that store owner. And the cops.

"You're insane. You really think that would be fun?"

"Sort of."

Jason looked at me like I'd just admitted I wanted to try out for the lead role in *The Nutcracker.* "I guess everyone needs a goal in life. If that's what you want, go ask the guy."

"I told you, he's busy." There were too many people around right now. I didn't want to take a chance of getting shot down in front of a bunch of strangers. Besides, if you don't ask people for things, they can't say no.

"He isn't busy. Nobody wants to dunk the clown. He's already all wet. . . . Hey, mister," Jason called.

I grabbed his arm and dragged him away. He let me pull him, but he kept shouting until the tank was out of sight, "Mister! Mister Barker! My friend wants a job. Hey, mister. My friend's a real clown. I swear. He'd be perfect. We even call him Captain Clown. King Clown. Chad the Clown. He's the clown with a million names."

"Cut it out," I told him. "People are staring at us."

"Then stop dragging me."

I let go of his arm. "The other Bozo was really good," I said. "You'll see."

"I'm sure I will," Jason said. "We've got all summer."

He kept talking, but I tuned him out. There was something much more important ahead of us. Coming up, to the right, was the one thing that would make the difference between this being just another summer or maybe being the greatest summer of my life.

7

PAST WILD WILLY'S, THE BOARDWALK GREW WIDER. THERE were game booths and food stalls all along the ocean side. On the street side most of one block was filled with a big arcade attached to a fudge shop. Smart planning—while parents waited in line to buy fudge, their kids played video games.

Three booths stood around the arcade entrance. Two of them meant nothing to me. One, on the left, was a wheel. You bet on a number and pushed a button to start a big spinner, then pushed it again to stop the spinner. If you won, you got a box of candy. At a glance, the odds looked pretty good. Six numbers were painted really big around the center of the wheel. But if you followed the lines between them, the actual winning space was real small. And each number was painted in two colors, splitting it in half. So, to win, you didn't just have to pick number five, for example, but blue five and not white five. All together, the wheel had eighteen different numbers crammed around the outer rim. With two colors on each number, the odds against winning were thirty-six to one. At fifty cents a chance, you'd spend an average of eighteen dollars to win a five-dollar box of candy. Nice profit. But good odds or bad odds, I wasn't interested in candy.

The booth on the right side of the arcade was a water race. People competed against each other, trying to pop a balloon by shooting a stream of water into a target. It was an honest game, with a winner each time. You couldn't get the large prize unless there were enough players. Two to six players meant a small prize. Seven to ten meant medium. Eleven or twelve meant large. Since each person plunked down two bucks to play, the game raked in at least twenty-two dollars when a large prize was at stake. The prize probably cost them less than three bucks. Another nice profit. But I wasn't interested in popping balloons, either.

Between the wheel and the water race, in front of the arcade, was the Cat-a-Pult. That was the game I cared about. To play, you put a small stuffed cat in a little scoop at the top of a miniature catapult, pulled the shaft back, and let go. The cat flew through the air toward a group of metal buckets sitting on a rotating wooden disk. If you missed, but were close enough to hit the side of a bucket, someone working the game would usually shout, "Your cat kicked the bucket!" Sick, but sort of funny.

As an added touch, the disk was covered with sand. I guess it was supposed to make the place look like a beach, but I thought it looked more like a giant litter box. The game was the kind you could walk around, with five catapults set up on each of the four sides. The workers got real busy if there was a crowd. Speakers attached to the corners of the booth let loose with a taped cat yowl every half minute or so.

It wasn't hard to win, and you got three chances for a dollar. But there was a trade-up. One win earned you a small prize. You could trade three small prizes for a medium. Then three mediums for a large. In boardwalk language, *large* was nowhere near the end of the line. It went on from there up through extra large, giant, jumbo, and super. Yet another lesson for the mathematically challenged. I figured it out once. You'd need 729 small prizes to earn one super.

"Young love is so touching," Jason said as I scanned the booth.

"Cut it out. We were just friends." *Barely friends,* I thought. There was a chance she wouldn't even remember me. I remembered her. All fall. All winter. And all spring.

"She's not here," Jason said.

"I know. I can see that. Maybe she's coming later." *Or maybe she's not coming.*

"You going to stand there staring all night like a lost puppy?" Jason asked.

"Maybe."

He pointed at the two girls working the booth. "They'd probably be able to tell you whether she's around." The girls, both about my age, wore red T-shirts decorated with a black-and-white drawing of a rather startled cat sailing through the air.

I shook my head. "I'll check back later."

"No. You need to be put out of your misery." Jason walked up to one of the girls. "Hey, is there a young lady from Montana working here? About this tall," he said, holding his hand, palm down, against the middle of his chest. "Long red hair. Lousy taste in guys."

"Don't know. I just started today. Sorry." She shrugged and smiled at Jason.

"Thanks." He glanced back to me. "She doesn't know. She just started working here today. Sorry."

"I heard. Come on." I didn't want to give Jason a chance to say anything else.

Too late.

"Listen," Jason said to the girl, "if she shows up, tell her Chad was asking for her. Okay?"

"Sure."

"Don't forget. Chad. With a C. Rhymes with bad."

She nodded and went back to work.

"You jerk," I said, hitting Jason on the shoulder.

"You're welcome," he said. "Always happy to help a buddy. Hey, I just realized Chad rhymes with mad, too. And sad. And Trinidad." He turned around like he was going to share his discovery with the girl at the Cat-a-Pult.

I grabbed his arm and spun him back. As we walked toward Panic Pier at the midpoint of the boardwalk, my mind returned to last summer. She'd been there the whole season. But, just my luck, I didn't meet her until the end of August. Gwen O'Sullivan. From Montana. Last year, one happy day, I'd wandered past the Cat-a-Pult when a little boy was playing. He wasn't strong enough to get the cats anywhere near the buckets. This girl inside the booth was helping him, sort of guiding the cats through the air, making sure the boy won a prize. I stopped to watch.

The prizes hung from hooks along the top of the booth. The one the little kid wanted—a tiny plush turtle—was high up. The girl had to stand on the counter. As she grabbed for a turtle, she started to slip. I reached up and put a hand against her side, steadying her.

She clutched my arm for an instant as she caught her balance. A surge shot through my body, jolting my heart and robbing me of the ability to breathe. I felt like I'd made contact with a power line.

"Thanks," she said. I know this sounds corny, but her voice—even that one word—was like music. She plucked the prize from its clip and hopped back down to the ground.

"Sure." My own voice sounded like the croak of a frog. My body felt like it was made of liquid, with nothing but the thinnest layer of skin to keep me from flowing into a puddle across the boards at my feet.

Her eyes were green, with brown flecks.

"Here you go," she said, handing the stuffed turtle to the boy. She glanced back at me and said, "My hero."

Her red hair, laced with copper and gold, fell halfway down her back, shimmering like polished metal.

I drifted away, clueless of what more to say and afraid that if I opened my mouth nothing would come out but braying donkey cries.

The next day I walked past the Cat-a-Pult at least twenty times. She was always busy, working hard. I tried to catch her eye, but she never looked my way. The day after that I made the ultimate sacrifice. I dug out my money and played. For the first five dollars, I didn't say anything. As I handed her my sixth dollar, I tried to think of something clever.

"Nice game." *You dork*. That sounded so lame, I cringed.

But she smiled. Oh, lord, she had small dimples in her cheeks.

Somehow, by my tenth dollar, we were exchanging full sentences. To tell the truth, she was providing most of the full ones while I was building my way up from one word to two or three at a time. *Montana. Wow. Sounds cool. Like it there? Like it here?*

Montana seemed as far away as China. I'd never been to any state that didn't share a border with New Jersey. I'd never been anywhere that didn't look just like New Jersey.

Two days and thirty dollars later, I was actually talking with her—hanging out at the booth and chatting whenever she wasn't too busy. I found out she was staying with her cousin, who worked downtown.

The day after that we took a walk together during her break. For two more days we walked, while I listened to the music of her voice and tried to find the courage to ask her out. On the next afternoon, as we strolled along the boardwalk, I got ready to mention that there was a really good movie playing in the theater on Thirty-fourth Street. Before I could even start, she said, "Good-bye," and told me she had to go pack her suitcase. The morning after, as far as I knew, she got on a plane back to Montana. Or maybe China.

I'd never even thought to get her address. Gwen O'Sullivan. Short for Guinevere. "My dad's a big fan of King Arthur," she'd explained.

When she'd said good-bye, she'd said one other thing. "See you next year, Chad Turner."

Those words, and the memory of her voice, had carried me through three seasons.

Next year was finally here.

8

WHACK!

I jumped as Jason smacked me on the back of the head.

"Wake up," he said. "You look like a druggie."

"I was just thinking," I said. I noticed we'd covered more than a block while my mind had traveled back a year.

"Summer's no time for thinking," Jason said. "Save it for school."

That got my attention. "Pay up," I said, holding my hand out.

Jason groaned, then gave me a dollar. We had a rule—mention school during the summer and you owed a dollar. Mention a teacher's name, and it was two bucks. School didn't belong in any part of our summer.

We squeezed through the crowds by Panic Pier and then walked past Thrillville, the smallest of the ride piers, without running into any of our friends. Like everything else, the boardwalk came to an end. The crowds thinned out, the shops got smaller. After crossing a final stretch with no shops at all, we reached the southern end. I leaned against the railing for a minute, looking back at where I'd been, and tried to let the images fill my mind and push away all thoughts.

"Don't worry," Jason said. "She'll show up."

"Hope so."

"Ready to spend some money?"

"Sure."

We headed back north.

"How about a tattoo?" Jason asked. He stopped in front of the entrance to one of the seven zillion places that offered tattoos, henna, branding, piercing, and, for all I knew, emergency appendectomies.

"Right." I'd gotten an earring after the second time Dad split, when I was in sixth grade. Other than that, I hadn't had anything pierced or tattooed. Jason had a unicorn on his left shoulder, and he was always joking that I should get a tattoo. But the one time I was actually thinking about it, he'd told me he'd kill me if I went ahead.

Still, it didn't hurt to look. We stepped inside and checked out the samples on the wall. Incense burned my eyes and tickled my throat. I wondered if everything in the shop was supposed to cause pain. "The tiger," I said, pointing to a large Bengal. "Now that's me."

Jason shook his head and tapped a long-stemmed rose. *"That's* you." He leaned over and sniffed my head. "Yup. Definitely. With all the fertilizer in there, flowers would do great."

I gave him a shove and we moved along.

"Laser tag?" Jason asked as we passed near the entrance to the Galactic Zapper.

"Too expensive." It was great running around in the dark, shooting friends and strangers in the back, but at five bucks a game I didn't play too often. "Want to hit a few?"

Jason grinned. "Sure."

We went to the batting cages. I tried the seventy-mile-per-hour hardball. I only hit three out of twenty, and one of those popped straight up from the bat, nearly taking off my nose. That was more than enough for me. After the third hit, my hands were buzzing. Besides, I had a hard time concentrating. Stepping into the cage got me thinking about how it would feel to climb into the dunk tank. And a batting cage is a bad place to be when your mind is drifting.

Jason stuck with slow-pitch softball. He knocked nearly every ball straight out against the netting at the far end of the cage.

"It's no challenge when they come that slow," I said as I watched him bat a second round.

"It's no fun when they come that fast," he replied. He whacked a solid shot. "It would be like trying to hit off Stinger Dalton."

I thought about the kid from the baseball team at school with the awesome pitching arm. "I think he throws faster than these machines."

"Yeah," Jason nodded as he nailed his last ball. "It definitely wouldn't be much fun batting against him." He took off his helmet and stepped out of the cage.

On the way back we found Mike and Corey inside Panic Pier. They were standing under the sky ride. Mike was staring up at the girls as they passed overhead. So was Corey, though he was pretending not to.

"Pervert," Jason said, giving Mike a push.

"What's up?" I asked.

"Can't hang long," Mike said. "I'm on break."

"Whatcha working?" Jason asked.

"A wheel," Mike told him.

"I'm free," Corey said. He shrugged, then added, "I'm always free."

Something smelled strangely familiar but oddly out of place. "You wearing sunscreen?" I asked Corey.

He nodded. "Nothing wrong with being careful."

"It's dark," I told him.

"It wasn't when I left the house. You can laugh at me now, but in twenty years we'll see who's right. You guys are going to have faces like grilled steak."

"That's something to look forward to," Jason said.

"Mmm, steak," Mike said. He glanced at his watch, sighed, took one last lingering look up at the sky ride, then headed off to continue his shift at the game wheel.

"Heaven help us if he ever becomes a ride operator," Jason said.

"Heaven help the riders," I said. But the funny thing was, as sleazy as Mike could get, he was honest. A lot of guys would dip into the cash when they worked a booth. I knew how tempting that could be. There was really no way to catch someone who snuck a couple bucks. But Mike had his own code. He'd never steal from his boss. The couple times I worked a booth, filling in for someone who needed a quick break, I tried to touch the roll as little as possible. I was afraid if I took some money even once, it would become a habit.

We moved farther down the pier and hung out near the Cyclospin for a while, watching people stagger from the cars and try to walk straight as they came out of the exit.

"I'll sell you a ride," a familiar voice said from behind us.

I turned around and saw Anthony pull a plastic bag

partway out of his pants pocket, revealing a handful of white pills.

Jason leaned over and whispered something to Anthony, who shrugged and took off.

"What was that about?" I asked.

"I told him if he ever came near any of us with that junk again, I'd shove it so far up his ass he'd be able to taste it."

I wasn't sure whether to laugh or shudder at that image. "Just make sure you wear gloves."

"What a piece of walking scum," Corey said. "I can't believe he gets away with everything. If I sneeze, the teachers give me an angry look. Anthony could show up half loaded and everyone would think he was being cute."

"It's like he throws a switch whenever he wants, and people see this wonderful kid," I said. "They never realize it's all an act."

We talked for a while about the general unfairness of life. Then Jason and I headed back north. We'd invited Corey to join us, but he wanted to go home to do some work on his computer. I couldn't blame him. He was really good at it. He'd been making money designing webpages for people.

There was a bigger crowd by Wild Willy's now, clustered near the Bozo tank. We pushed our way through.

"Hey, blondie!" a rasping voice shouted at Jason.

I froze as I recognized the unmistakable sound of the good Bozo. Jason glanced over at the cage.

"Yeah, you, cheesehead. What did you do, dive into a vat of mayonnaise?"

"That's weird," Jason said to me. "I've got this sudden craving for a sandwich."

"I'd tell you a blond joke," the Bozo said, "but what's the point? You *are* a blond joke!"

The crowd laughed. And the Bozo unleashed his chain-saw cackle, "Hhhhhaaaaawwwwwhhhhoooooheeeeeeeyyaaaa!" I flinched in sympathy, but I knew Jason wasn't going to let it bother him. The Bozo was wasting his time on this vic. He might as well have been hurling his insults into an empty room. But he kept going. "Let's make America beautiful, folks. Somebody buy that kid a hat."

I couldn't believe it when Jason turned around and handed two bucks to the barker.

Thwunk!

He barely missed.

"Could someone explain the instructions to blondie?" the Bozo asked. "Help him with the big words, like HIT THE TARGET!"

Thwunk!

Another close one.

"Better give it up, kid. You've got about as much chance of doing this as—"

Thwank! Splash!

Jason nailed the target. People cheered and hooted. The Bozo scampered back up and started taunting his next mark.

"Good shot," I said. "You angry?"

"Nah. I was going to just walk away, but I figure the guy works hard in there, so why not spend a couple bucks. It's kind of like with your mom."

"What are you talking about?" An image of my mom in the tank flashed through my mind. What could she shout? *Make your bed! Finish your homework! Eat your vegeta-*

bles! That didn't work. It was about as ridiculous as trying to picture Jason in a ballerina skirt.

"You know—tips. People go to a restaurant and they get a good waitress like your mom who does everything just fine. Maybe even does more than they expected. So it wouldn't hurt them to kick in an extra buck or two for the tip. But lots of them don't."

Yeah. I knew what he meant. Mom didn't complain much, but I could tell there were days when she wasn't happy with her job. Sometimes she'd work really hard taking care of a table and they wouldn't leave any tip. That sucked.

"Now what?" Jason asked.

It was too early to go back home. And I was right where I wanted to be. But if I admitted that, Jason would start kidding me again. "I don't know. I guess we could hang out here. Want to watch the Bozo for a while?" I asked, trying to sound like I wasn't all that interested.

Jason shrugged. "If that's how you get your kicks. But let's back off a bit."

"Good idea."

We stood to the side of the crowd.

"Hey," the Bozo shouted at a guy wearing a big gold chain and a shirt that was unbuttoned halfway down his chest. "Look who broke away from his leash."

The mark's head snapped toward the tank. This was great. Guys like that always acted like they were better than anyone else. Once, I was just looking through the window of this Corvette parked on Ninth Street, trying to check out the dashboard, when the owner ran up and shouted at me to get away from it. He had a lot of gold on him, too.

"Please, if you're not going to button that shirt, at least comb your chest before you leave the house," the Bozo said.

Twelve bucks later, Mr. Chain got his revenge.

A cluster of sullen girls went by, all wearing black clothing, black nail polish, black lipstick, black eye makeup, and black hair streaked with colors normally seen only in comic books. They were the kind of girls who usually stared right through me. I'd have given almost anything for a chance to be in the tank at that moment. It would have been so great to lean into the microphone and let loose. The Bozo had a field day. "Wow. Didn't know they ran a late shift at the coal mine. Next time, WASH YOUR FACE!" That was just for starters. By the time he was done with them, each girl had taken a couple turns.

"Doesn't this strike you as kind of cruel?" Jason asked as the girls headed off, laughing and poking each other.

"Nope." I figured people got insulted all day in big and small ways anyhow. It was part of life. In school, at work, in stores—even on the street if you ran into the wrong cop. At least here you had a chance to get even. I pointed at the girls. "They don't look injured, do they?"

"I guess not," Jason said.

I turned my attention back to the Bozo. Nobody was spared—men, women, boys, girls. Say what you will about the insults, the Bozo didn't play favorites. He nailed everyone. The thing that really blew me away was how I never heard him say the same thing twice. Except for his laugh. He let loose with that a whole lot.

I also learned he could do more than just strike out with words. At one point, this guy who missed with a bunch of throws ran toward the target. I guess he wanted to push it and dunk the Bozo that way. The barker didn't even try to stop him. He just grinned. A second later, right before the guy reached the target, I found out the reason for the grin. The Bozo slid smoothly off the ledge into the water. He didn't go under like when he was dunked. Instead, he plunged both hands down in front of him and splashed a double scoop of slimy water at the guy, nailing him in the face.

The guy stood there for a moment, drenched, while the crowd laughed at him and clapped for the Bozo. I could tell he wanted to get even, but there was nothing he could do. Finally, he slunk off down the boardwalk. The Bozo was unbeatable. He had a microphone, he had iron bars, he had makeup. And if you tried to run up and smack the target, he had that covered, too.

The more I watched, the more I wanted a turn. Out here in the world, you never knew what would happen when you opened your mouth. Someone might laugh. Or throw a punch. Or just ignore you. In the tank, it was different. People loved the Bozo. And nobody ignored him. Nobody looked down on him or told him he was a loser.

Finally, near eleven, as the crowds started to thin, the Bozo swung out a section of the bars and climbed through an opening at the back of the tank. Another Bozo—the bad one we'd seen earlier—waddled from a door at the side of a building behind the right corner of the tank, about twenty feet away. The good Bozo headed there.

"The changing of the Bozos," Jason said. "I've heard all about it, but I never dreamed I'd live to see the ceremony. Oh, I wish I had my camera." He turned to a guy standing next to him. "Hey, got a camera? Someone really should take a picture of this."

"Think so?" the guy asked, his eyebrows rising a good half inch.

"Absolutely."

"Marge," the guy said, tapping his wife on the shoulder. "Get me the camera, quick."

"I thought you had the camera," she said.

They started to argue about who had the camera. I stopped paying attention to them. Something about the Bozo caught my eye. For a moment, as I watched, it didn't really sink in. Why did he look so familiar? Then I knew the answer. And the answer really pissed me off.

9

"IT'S *HIM*," I SAID.

"Who?" Jason asked.

"The new tenant. The guy my mom just rented the apartment to." I glared at the Bozo as he limped up to the dressing-room door and went inside. I couldn't believe I'd thought he was so great. "I'm sure it's him."

"Cool. You've got the Bozo living with you. Maybe he can teach you how to be mean and nasty. I understand it's a great way to pick up girls. 'Hey, you with the big nose, wanna dance?' I can see where that would be a real turn-on."

"You don't understand." I explained how the jerk had sat on the bench and not done a thing to help me while I was getting into trouble with the cops.

"They didn't arrest you," Jason said. "It's over with. So what's the problem?"

"Nothing. Forget it. Come on." I turned my back on the tank and headed away from the pier. "Let's go to your place, okay?"

"Sure."

Jason lived on Sea Crest, too, three blocks past my house. He had his own room upstairs. No tenants. His dad owned a roofing business, and his mom did some kind of accounting for the township. It's funny—Jason worked all year except for the summer, and his dad worked all year except for the winter.

Mike's folks were off schedule, too. Mike's dad worked the night shift at a factory and his mom worked days as a receptionist, so they didn't see each other much. Sometimes work really got in the way of life.

I thought of another pair that didn't match up. My mom worked day and night. She seemed to need to keep busy. When he was around, my dad couldn't hold a job. I pushed that memory out of my mind. I was angry enough already.

We hung out in Jason's room for a while listening to CDs. The volume was cranked, but after hours wading through the jumble of noises from the boardwalk, the music seemed almost peaceful.

Around midnight I headed home. Mom was already in bed, so I was careful not to make any noise. As I fell asleep, I could hear the idiot pacing around upstairs. Maybe he spent his nights inventing stuff to say in the tank. Whatever was going on up there, I wanted nothing to do with him. I couldn't believe I'd wasted so much time watching the freak. If I'd known who it was behind the makeup, I'd have walked right by the first time. Now that I thought about it, he really wasn't all that great. I'd bet a lot of people could have done the same thing. The makeup was a big part of it. So was the tank. And the microphone. Anyone would sound cool shouting through those speakers.

But I still wanted a shot at being the Bozo. I knew, deep in my gut, that I'd be good. Better than him. A lot better. Sitting there, behind the bars, behind the face paint, I could let loose at anyone I felt like nailing. Snobs, nasty teachers, people who didn't care about their kids—I'd get them all.

In my mind, nobody ever hit the target.

Finally, counting marks the way other people might have counted sheep, I drifted off.

I woke early enough to make breakfast for me and Mom. She could get a meal at the diner, but I knew she wouldn't have time to eat once the rush started.

"Delicious," she said as we finished our eggs. "So what'd you do last night?"

"The usual. Hit the boardwalk with Jason. Robbed a couple banks. Got my eyeball pierced. If I had a job, I could avoid all sorts of danger."

"Don't start. It's too early in the day."

"Sorry." I glared out the window as I heard the clump of footsteps on the apartment stairs.

Mom opened the front door. "Mr. Vale," she called.

The clown from the tank came to the doorway. "Good morning."

"Good morning." Mom pointed at me. "This is my son, Chad."

He nodded and smiled. "It's a pleasure to meet you."

"Chad, this is Mr. Vale." She glanced back at him. "Or is it Professor?" The touch of respect in her voice made me sick. She'd dropped out of school as soon as she was old enough—thanks mostly to Dad. She'd made up for it later, studying and taking that test where you get the same thing as a diploma. Since then she'd been signing up for one kind of course or another for as long as I could remember. None of it had gotten us anywhere. She'd studied how to cut hair, but that hadn't worked out. The one time she cut mine, it looked pretty bad. Some kid at school had made a joke about it and we'd gotten into a fight. He didn't look too good after that, either.

Next she'd started a course in helping people do their taxes, but numbers weren't her best thing. Then she'd tried dental assistant. And other stuff. She'd stuck with the latest class longer than any of the others. During all that time in all those schools, she'd developed this extreme respect for instructors.

"Just call me Malcolm," the Bozo said. His voice was nowhere near the rasping snarl he used in the tank. To tell the truth, he sounded like a college professor. All that was missing was one of those tweed jackets they wear. He stepped inside and held out his hand toward me, acting like we'd never met before.

At least he didn't say anything about my problem with the cops. That was a break. Whenever I'd gotten in trouble, Mom had overreacted. She was kind of spooked about cops because of the couple times way back when they'd showed up at the house looking for Dad. Still, no matter what this freak could tell her about me, I wanted to spit in his hand. But Mom would really flip if I did that. Nice boys don't go spitting on professors. So I gritted my teeth and shook hands with him.

Mom glanced over at the clock. "I'd better run," she said. She gave me a quick kiss on the cheek. "Be good. I'll see you after work."

"Bye."

"So long, Mrs. Turner," Malcolm said.

She smiled at him. "Call me Annie."

I watched her dash out. Malcolm was still there, standing by the table.

"Professor?" I asked. "Of what? Dunkology? Insultosophy?"

"Very clever." He smiled at me like we were old friends. "Amusing as it may seem, it's the truth. I'll be teaching theater arts at Baldwin Community College in the fall. Right now I'm working at my summer job."

"I know. I saw you." I searched his face carefully and spotted a small dab of clown makeup at the edge of his jaw under his right ear.

"And I saw you. With your large blond friend."

"Jason," I said. I was about to tell him more when I caught myself. He wasn't going to sucker me into a friendly conversation. I didn't have any plans to become buddies with this clown. Not after the way he'd tried to screw me with the cops. "Look, I've got to get going. Okay?"

"Something wrong?" he asked. "Have I offended you?"

I didn't answer. It was none of his business. I could tell he was trying to get on my good side. That wasn't going to happen. I figured he was like an adult version of Anthony— all slick and charming when he wanted something.

"Oh, I get it," he said. "Yesterday. With the sunglasses and that rather angry gentleman from the shop. Is that what you're sulking about?" He pushed out his lower lip like a pouting child.

"No." I was going to turn away from him, but the words tumbled from my mouth. "Yeah. You're right, I'm angry." Now that I'd let it out, I couldn't stop. "You should have said something. You know I didn't steal anything. But you just sat there. You didn't help me. That really stinks." I felt my face grow hot, flamed by the memories.

"You were doing fine on your own. You didn't need any help from me. They let you go, right?"

I glared at him.

"Right?" he asked again.

"You still could have helped me."

He shook his head. "No way. It was too good a scene to break up."

Now I was completely lost. "You really suck. You know that, *Professor?* And it wasn't any kind of scene, whatever that means."

"Sure it was. Everything's a scene. As the Bard once said, 'All the world's a stage.'" He turned his head to the side for a moment, then snapped it back in my direction. His eyes flashed with fear. "I didn't take anything." He spread out his arms and looked around in terror. Then he pointed a shaking finger in the direction of an empty chair. "You saw it, didn't you? I was here the whole time."

Oh, man. That was me, when I was grabbed by the cops. My words. My motions. I felt like I'd been cloned. It made me sick. I remember once, in the mall, I'd glanced across the corridor and my eyes had locked on a person who looked just like me. It had taken me a moment to realize I was staring at a mirror, but in the instant before everything fell back into place, I'd been filled with the weirdest sense that there was something wrong with reality. This was just as bad. Maybe worse. "Stop that!" I yelled. "You think it's some kind of joke?"

"You think it's some kind of joke?" he shouted back, his face reflecting my anger like a mirror made of flesh.

I wanted to smash that face. I wanted to slam my fist into his mouth and shut it forever. The crazy thought shot through my mind that if I hit him, I'd hurt myself—like he was some sort of life-size voodoo doll. "What kind of freak are you?" I asked.

The angry kid melted away. "The saddest kind," he said, sounding like a normal man again.

"You're crazy."

"Crazy?" His eyes flashed with madness. "They all said I was crazy, but I'll have the last laugh."

I took a step away from him, afraid he was about to totally lose control.

"Pretty good, huh?" he asked. Just like that, the crazy face faded. The professor face was back. "Crazy is easy. Try it. Come on. My gut tells me you can do it. Dig into your experiences and show me crazy."

"I'm not showing you anything."

He shook his head. "Yeah, crazy is too easy. Anyone can do that. You want a challenge? Try something subtle, like curiosity mixed with revulsion. Or slightly jealous with a tinge of hate. Now, those take some skill. Or a community college professor. Talk about a challenging role."

"How about screaming insults from inside a cage?" I asked. "Does that take skill?"

"Maybe. Maybe not. Depends on what gifts you're born with. Sadly, my fellow Bozo, Waldo, to take a rather obvious example, has very little skill. He tries his best. I'm sure you've seen him at work. That's beside the point. Mock the job if you will—you're not fooling me. I saw you last night. You liked the show. You liked it a whole lot. The eyes don't lie." He glanced at the clock. "Well, I'll leave you to whatever you were doing." He opened the door.

"Yeah, get out of here," I muttered. I couldn't believe it.

What a stuck-up lunatic. He was like some kind of vampire, except instead of sucking blood, he sucked up people's emotions for his own use. That was really sick.

Right then Jason showed up, his volleyball tucked under his right arm. He and Malcolm exchanged glances and nodded the way strangers do when they suspect they have something in common. Then Malcolm left, but when he reached the sidewalk, he spun back and said, "Hey, does either of you have a van?"

I didn't answer. I wouldn't even turn sixteen until the end of August. I was just about the youngest kid in my class. And all we had was Mom's third-hand Civic. Even if I had a truck and a license, I wouldn't do this creep any favors.

"My dad needs the van for work, but my folks let me use the Blazer," Jason said. "Except I just have my permit. I can't drive unless there's someone along with a license. At least, I'm not supposed to." He winked at me.

Jason and I had taken a couple midnight spins around the block. That stopped one night when his dad caught us pulling up to the curb. I'd expected Jason to get grounded for life, but his dad just held his hand out for the keys and said, "It might be a good idea for you to wait until that's legal."

"Perfect," Malcolm said. "I have a license. Listen, I need to get my things. They're just up the Parkway at that U-Store place off the next exit. I'll pay you to help. Ten dollars each? How's that sound?"

"You've got a deal," Jason said before I could turn down the offer. "I don't live far from here. We can walk over and get the Blazer whenever you want."

"Meet you here around two?" Malcolm asked.

Jason nodded, and Malcolm walked off.

The mention of money reminded me of something. "What about the rent?" I called after him.

His answer drifted over his shoulder. "I'll have it to-morrow."

10

"ALL RIGHT," JASON SAID AS I CLOSED THE DOOR. "TEN EASY bucks each. I like this guy."

"You haven't even met the real him," I said.

"What are you talking about? He was right here."

"Never mind." I didn't feel like going into it.

Jason switched topics. "Beach?" he asked, tossing the volleyball up like he was getting ready to serve. He swatted at it, and I flinched, imagining the destructive path the ball would take through the room. But he swung wide and let the ball drop into his open hand. "Well?"

"Sure. For a bit."

We went down to the closest nets, right off the boardwalk by Ninth Street. There were games at two of the three courts. A group of vacationers was playing a clumsy but enthusiastic battle with six people on one side and seven on the other. No passing, no setups, no teamwork—just whapping the ball back and forth. It was more like gang tennis than anything else. The serious players, mostly college-age, were running two-man teams in a round robin. Jason fit right in. He was an awesome player. He hooked up with one of the college guys he knew, Franco, and they took on every challenger.

I plunked down off to the side of the courts, where I

watched the action and thought about using Malcolm's head for a volleyball.

Eventually, a voice broke into my fantasies. "Getting a nice workout?"

I looked over my shoulder. It was Ellie, in her lifeguard suit, with her whistle around her neck. "I'm pacing myself," I said. "You on a break?"

She nodded and squatted down next to me. "Figured you guys might be here. How's he playing?"

"Better than ever," I said.

We watched for a while, making occasional comments about Jason's performance on the court. Ellie was one of those friends I could hang out with in comfortable silence—we didn't need to talk. It was just nice having her around.

After about fifteen minutes, she glanced at her watch and stood up. "Got to go. Guess you'll have to take over."

"I think I can handle it."

"Try not to strain anything." She headed back to her lifeguard chair.

When I got tired of sitting I caught Jason's attention and said, "I'm going to hit the boardwalk."

Jason nodded, paused to catch his breath, then said, "Sure. See you around two."

"Great." I left the beach and strolled toward Doc's arcade.

A different Bozo was working the tank. I watched him for a minute. He wasn't as bad as the other one, but he wasn't all that good, either. A few people got annoyed enough at his insults to pay for a chance to dunk him, but most folks just walked right past. I knew I could do better.

"Where'd you get that haircut, kid?" the Bozo called.

I ignored him and went over to the barker.

"Two bucks," the barker said, holding out three balls in one hand. He didn't even bother to look at me.

"That's a really ugly haircut," the Bozo said. "What'd you use, a lawn mower?"

I took a deep breath. Sometimes it was so hard to ask people for things, especially strangers. And especially things I really wanted. But this was just two words. A lot shorter than *Would you like to go to a movie?*

"You hiring?" I asked. I wanted to say more. I wanted to tell him how bad most of his Bozos were. And how good I'd be.

He looked at me now and grinned, revealing clues of past meals clinging to his teeth. I noticed more food smears on the front of his shirt. Even out in the fresh air, I caught a strong whiff of clothing badly in need of a tub of soapy water. "Yeah, I got an opening." He pulled a piece of beef jerky from his shirt pocket and tore off a bite.

"Really?" It came out as a shout.

"Really." He stared at me for a moment as he chewed the jerky. "You a hard worker?"

"The best. You can ask anyone. Doc at the arcade will tell you. Or Salvatore at the pizzeria. Ask anyone. Dependable, too."

"It's a tough job. Most guys I hire don't last."

"I'll last," I promised. "You have my word."

"We'll see." He wiped his right hand on his jeans, then held it out. "My name's Bob. You can call me Boss."

"Chad," I said, shaking his hand. His grip felt greasy.

"Be here tonight at seven," he told me.

"Great. I'll see you then." I headed off, my heart pounding like someone was trying to kick it out of my chest. Seven. I wondered whether he was going to give me Malcolm's spot. That would show him. Maybe Malcolm had messed up. This was so excellent! I couldn't wait to tell Jason.

No. I wouldn't tell him. I grinned as I realized how I'd play it. I'd ask him to meet me in front of Wild Willy's tonight. When he got near the tank, I'd let him have it. I'd nail him with all kinds of personal stuff. He'd freak. It would be so cool. He'd go crazy trying to figure out how some clown knew all about him. It would be like the Psychic Bozo Network. Man, maybe I could surprise Mike and Corey, too.

When I was about ten feet away from the tank, I thought of something. "Hey," I called back, shouting to get Bob's attention, "what should I wear?"

He shrugged. "Something you don't mind getting wet."

Duh. I guess that made sense. No problem there. Anyone who lived near the ocean had plenty of stuff that could get wet. I had a blue long-sleeved T-shirt. And thin nylon pants. There'd be clown makeup in that room next to the tank. Otherwise, the guy would've told me to buy some. They probably hired new Bozos all the time, so they'd have to keep supplies on hand.

I walked along, picking out people and practicing in my head the things I'd shout when I was in the tank. I knew I was going to do a great job tonight.

Job? Oh, man. I swore out loud as I realized what I'd done. If I asked Mom for permission, she'd say no. If I didn't ask, I'd be sneaking behind her back. But I didn't have to tell her today. I could wait a couple days. Get real good at it, then have her come see me. If I was absolutely wonderful, she'd have to say it was okay. She was always trying to get me to do stuff in school like go out for the play or learn an instrument. This wasn't any different.

I swung by the Cat-a-Pult on the way to Doc's. Gwen wasn't there. Maybe she was working at a different booth. Or maybe she'd be coming later in the summer. I hoped she'd come soon.

"Hey, my favorite gofer. Where you been?" Doc asked when I reached the arcade.

"Around. Need anything?"

"Desperately." He pulled a wad of bills out of his pocket and peeled off a faded ten. "Get me a double sausage sandwich from Strombo's, and a large coffee. Black."

I took the money. "Be right back."

"Tell him not to give you the stuff that's been sitting out since yesterday," Doc yelled after me.

"No problem."

I got Doc his sandwich.

"Whatcha have left, one year of school?" Doc asked when I gave him the bag.

"Two," I told him.

He glared across the room and shouted at a couple kids who were shaking one of the iron-claw machines, then looked back at me. "And after that? Got plans?"

I shrugged. "Maybe California."

"That's not a plan. That's a state."

"Yeah. I know. But it's a state where the boardwalk arcades are open all year round."

Doc grunted. I couldn't tell whether that meant he agreed with my comment or thought it was totally absurd.

"Down the road, you ever need a full-time job, come see me."

"Thanks."

"I hired your dad at least twice," Doc said.

From what I remembered, my dad had worked for just about everybody around here. But never very long at any one place.

"Got a confession," Doc said. "I think I fired him at least twice, too."

"I figured." This wasn't a subject I felt like exploring. But there was something else I wanted to ask Doc. "Hey, that guy you told about the apartment. Malcolm. Is he a friend of yours? He seems kind of crazy."

"I met him last fall when I went fishing in Texas. He was working the southern carnival route. He's weird, but he's not dangerous." Doc turned away to shout at a kid who was kicking the change machine.

"Where's he from? Is he really a teacher? Has he been a Bozo for long?"

"What do I look like? The History Channel? Stop asking so many questions." Doc scanned the arcade, then walked over to the old Street Fighter game, his belt jangling with a cluster of keys that must have weighed fifteen pounds. He opened the front panel of the machine and clicked a switch until I had a bunch of credits. "Here. Waste some more of your life. My treat."

"Thanks." I realized Doc was finished chatting. I played until I used all the credits. By then it was time to head back.

Gwen still wasn't at the Cat-a-Pult. Not that I was obsessed or anything.

The air was heating up, getting pretty warm for this

time of year. It felt even warmer because there was almost no breeze. The last thing I wanted to do right now was move boxes. I really didn't feel like helping Malcolm, but I couldn't let Jason down. Besides, I had this funny feeling that if I didn't go along, Jason and Malcolm would be best friends by the next time I saw them.

Maybe they already were.

I found them sitting together on the upstairs porch when I got home. Jason leaned on the railing above me. "Hey, Chad, did you know Malcolm is going to teach at Baldwin this fall?"

"I heard. Come on. Let's get this over with."

They came down and we walked over to Jason's house. He got the keys from inside, then unlocked the Blazer. Malcolm climbed in the back. I rode up front with Jason. I think the person with the license was supposed to be in front, but it didn't matter. Jason was a good driver. He swore he was driving in New York when he was ten. The way he handled himself in traffic, I believed him.

"You win them all?" I asked as we headed down the road.

He nodded and told me the high points of his games. Behind us, Malcolm didn't say anything, which was fine with me.

"So what'd you do after you left?" Jason asked.

I nearly blurted out the news about the Bozo job before I remembered my plan to surprise Jason. He wasn't the only one in for a surprise. I glanced back at Malcolm, who was staring out the side window, looking sad. I almost felt sorry for him. But I realized that his expression had nothing to do with his feelings. He could switch on anything. If he wanted us to think he was sad, that's the way he'd act. I didn't see how anybody could trust a person who could fake his emotions so easily.

I turned away and passed the time telling Jason the highlights of my Street Fighter session. He listened, but he kept his eyes on the road, especially when we merged onto the Parkway.

The next exit wasn't far, and the U-Store place was right off the ramp. "It's nothing heavy," Malcolm said as Jason pulled into the parking lot. "Mostly boxes."

A lot of boxes, it turned out. We crammed as many cartons as we could in the back of the Blazer and stacked the rest of the stuff on one side of the rear seat. From the sound of them, half the boxes were probably filled with videotapes. There was also a small TV—the kind with a built-in VCR.

"This shouldn't take long," Jason said as he pulled up to the curb at my house. He hopped out and opened the back of the Blazer. Malcolm went ahead to unlock the door.

Jason and I each grabbed a box and followed him. It felt weird going upstairs. I mean, this was part of the house, but as long as someone else was paying rent, the apartment really wasn't part of my home.

Other than some furniture my mom had bought—a couch, a kitchen table, and two chairs—there wasn't much of anything inside the living room.

"You can stack them over there," Malcolm said, pointing to the bare wall opposite the couch.

Jason put down his box and stood for a moment, breathing like he'd run all the way back from the U-Store. "You okay?" I asked.

He nodded. "I'm fine. Just kind of hot."

"Sit down," Malcolm said. "Chad and I can get the rest of it."

"Yeah." I hated to agree with him, but he was right. Jason looked washed out. "We can handle it from here."

Jason shook his head. "I'm fine." He jogged down the stairs and grabbed another box from the Blazer. Then, I guess to show how fine he was feeling, he stacked a second box on top of the first.

I only took one for myself. Even that turned out to be almost too much. Jason was halfway up the steps, and I was right behind him, when he collapsed.

I BARELY MANAGED TO DROP MY BOX AND REACH UP IN TIME. Jason's damp T-shirt smacked against my palms. As I toppled backward under his weight, I shot out my right hand and grabbed the railing. I couldn't hold him without falling, so I moved down a couple steps and tried to lower him gently.

Malcolm rushed out to the porch. "Hang on!" he cried, racing down to meet us. He pulled the two boxes off Jason, tossing them up to the porch, then helped get him to a sitting position on the steps. The box I'd dropped had already tumbled to the ground.

"Guess I slipped," Jason said. He leaned against the railing.

"You're sweating like crazy," I said. "I think you're sick."

Jason shook his head. "Just hot. That's all."

"I'll get you a cold drink," Malcolm told him. He went back upstairs.

"What happened?" I asked. "Something's wrong. You're about as pale as beach sand."

"I'm fine," Jason insisted. "I must have a bug or something. No big deal."

Malcolm came back. "Go inside and sit," he said as he handed Jason a carton of orange juice.

I watched Jason get up, ready to grab him if he stumbled, but he kept his balance. I flinched when I thought about where he would have landed if I hadn't been there to catch him. Or where we both would have landed if my vision had been blocked by a second box.

"This ever happen to him before?" Malcolm asked me when we reached the bottom of the steps.

"Nope. Jason's so healthy he makes me sick sometimes."

Malcolm gave me a puzzled look.

"You know what I mean." I wasn't in the mood for friendly chatter. I grabbed the box I'd dropped, and shook it to see if anything had broken. In answer, I heard tinkling. I opened the flap. The box was crammed with books and magazines, but there was also a diploma in a thin black frame wedged between the books. It was from some place I'd never heard of, called Juilliard. The glass was cracked and a couple pieces had fallen off. "This broke," I told Malcolm as he walked past me.

He glanced down, then said, "It's not important."

Fine with me. I put the diploma back, closed the box and carried it upstairs. "You gonna live?" I asked Jason, who was sitting on the edge of the couch.

"Absolutely," he said. "I feel fine. Honest. I must have slipped or something." He stood up.

"Just stay there," I said. He really was looking better, but I figured he shouldn't take any chances. I gave him a light push. He plopped back down on the couch without any resistance.

We finished unloading. Then Malcolm drove the Blazer back to Jason's house.

After we'd all stepped out, Malcolm pulled two tens from his pocket. "Here you go."

I didn't want his money. But it would be more of a hassle to turn it down than to take it. "You should rest up," I told Jason.

"Yeah, maybe for a bit. I'll catch you later," he said.

"Okay." I started walking back home.

Malcolm headed that way, too. He walked next to me, but I ignored him. I checked my watch. It was almost four. In three hours I'd be working in the tank. I realized that if Malcolm lost his job, things at home would improve immediately: He wouldn't be able to pay the rent, and then he'd have to move.

Unless he talked Mom into letting him stay for free. He'd already conned her into waiting for the rent. I thought about the way he changed roles so easily. With that talent, how hard would it be to make her feel sorry for him? Hell, he could probably get free meals, too, if he put his mind to it. Next thing I knew, she'd order me to bring him breakfast in bed. Of course, Mom wasn't a pushover. Every once in a while there'd be some guy trying to ask her out. She usually turned them down gently. Except for the jerks. She'd tell them she didn't need another deadbeat in her life. *One to a customer.* That's what she'd say. But this guy, he'd probably try to fool her.

"You don't like me, do you?" he asked.

I realized I'd been glaring at him. "What was your first clue?"

"Look, I guess we got off to a bad start. Maybe I should have helped you with the cops yesterday."

I shrugged and muttered, "Forget about it. I don't need your help." I wasn't going to let him off that easily.

"I'll keep that in mind for the next time," he said.

"There won't be a next time. Just stay out of my business." I looked away from him as I spoke. Not to hide my anger, but to hide my smile. I realized that I sure wasn't going to stay out of his business. Just the opposite. I was about to get into his business in a big way.

12

MOM WAS AT THE KITCHEN TABLE, STUDYING.

"Test?" I asked.

She nodded.

"Better you than me." I went to the fridge and got a glass of milk, which I improved with a nice long squirt of chocolate syrup.

"I think it's going to be a tough one," she said.

"Stop worrying. You'll do fine." I realized that I was telling her the exact same thing she always told me before my tests. I just hoped my prediction turned out to be more accurate than hers were.

"How was your day?" Mom asked.

Different from usual, I thought. *Made ten bucks off a guy I hate, got the job of my dreams, and saved my best friend from rolling down the stairs and breaking his neck.* None of which was the kind of information a mom would be glad to hear—especially not the job part—so I settled for telling her, "Fine, so far."

"I saw you coming up the walk with Professor Vale. He seems like a very nice man."

I nodded. "Yup. He seems that way." I shut up and let her get back to studying. I knew that among the thousand other things she worried about, she was concerned I didn't have any father figures in my life. Well, that's one role Malcolm was never going to play.

I wanted to call Jason and tell him to meet me at Wild Willy's. But I realized he might be sleeping. He'd looked really wiped out when he'd gone into his house. I figured I'd probably have to wait until tomorrow to surprise him. Though there was a chance I'd still see him. Even if I didn't call him, he might come looking for me if he felt better.

As Mom was getting ready to leave for school, she asked me, "Got any plans for tonight?"

Oh, man. I couldn't lie. I remembered all the times she'd asked Dad, *Where are you going?* He'd tell her, *Just down to the corner for cigarettes.* He'd come home hours later, or maybe the next day.

"I figured I'd put on clown makeup and shout at people," I said.

Mom smiled and shook her head. "Very funny. That's what I get for asking." She rarely went to the boardwalk and had probably never paid any attention to the dunk tank.

"It's the latest fad," I told her, feeling a stab of guilt.

After she left, I went back out, hoping to kill time until seven. I thought about hanging around the dunk tank, but I really didn't want to stand there watching someone else when my own turn was so close. It would be like waiting on deck for a couple hours while another player batted.

First I checked the Cat-a-Pult. No familiar faces. I headed closer to the center, where I spotted Mike running the peach-basket game. I threw him a salute, in honor of his plans to join the army after graduation. He nodded, then went back to work. It was amazing to watch him in action. A guy walked past with his girlfriend. The girl was carrying a couple tiny teddy bears—the kind you got for hitting your number at the Lucky Aces wheel over by Panic Pier. I wondered how many tries it had taken to win them. The guy didn't even look over, but the girl did. She stopped and pointed at one of the prizes—a huge, fuzzy Pink Panther.

"That's soooooo adorable," she said.

"Yeah, adorable," the guy mumbled.

"I want it," she told him. It's amazing how a ninety-pound girl can control a hundred-eighty-pound guy with a small tug on the arm. "Win it for me, Rick."

"Come on, give it a try, Rick," Mike said, pouncing on the personal information. "Easiest thing on the planet. Get two in, ya win." He held up a pair of softballs in one hand and waved his other hand across the prizes displayed behind him. "One win gets you your choice, Rick."

"You can do it," the girl said.

The mark handed over a twenty and got his change. Poor guy. I figured Mike would work him for the whole bill.

The guy took careful aim, bent his knees to get a better angle, and gently tossed the first ball at the basket in front of him. It was the standard game. Nothing rigged. Nothing going against the player except the laws of physics. The basket is on its side, tilted up at a shallow angle. If you lob the ball so it barely lands inside the rim, and add a ton of backspin, it'll roll down and maybe stay in. Actually, there are a couple ways to toss it. But anything less than the perfect angle and spin, and the ball bounces right out. The bottom of the basket is really springy. As Corey had once described it, the player had to fight a losing battle against gravity *and* elasticity.

Naturally, the mark's first ball hit the bottom and shot right back out. He shook his head and tossed the second ball. If you miss the first time, the second turn is pointless, since you need two in to win.

"It's impossible. Let's get out of here." He turned away.

"Hey, Rick," Mike called, his voice slightly hushed.

The mark glanced back over his shoulder.

"C'mere," Mike said, motioning the guy closer.

"What?" The guy turned toward Mike.

"Look, Rick, you just had some bad luck that time. It could happen to anyone." He picked up a ball and tossed it in. From where he was standing behind the counter, it was easy to throw the ball so it stayed in the basket.

But that wasn't the real trick. That was just part of the preparation. I watched as Mike set the hook.

"Come on," he said, holding out another ball. He glanced nervously to each side, like he was worried that he'd get in trouble if his boss spotted what he was about to do. He spoke so softly I had to read his lips. "Listen, Rick, I'll give you a free practice throw."

That got the guy's attention. As he walked back to the counter, his expression changed. Suspicion gave way to greed.

"Free?" he asked. I guess he wanted to make sure he wasn't being scammed. "No catch?"

"Cross my heart," Mike said, making the appropriate gesture. "My treat. Just don't tell anyone, or you'll get me fired. I can trust you, can't I, Rick?"

The guy snatched the ball from Mike's outstretched hand. Who wouldn't? He leaned forward and tossed it toward the basket, just like before. It landed about three inches below the rim and rolled to the bottom. And, of course, this time it stayed there. Hard for it not to, since Mike had left the other ball in the basket. That kept the second one from bouncing out, making the game look easy.

"You did it!" the girl said, giving the guy's arm a squeeze.

"Yeah." The guy looked real proud as he dug for his wallet. "Okay. One more try."

Mike took out the two balls and handed them back to the guy. This was getting too painful to watch. I knew that even if the guy lucked out and managed to keep his first toss in the basket, Mike would remove the ball before the guy made his second toss. Odds are, the Pink Panther wasn't going anywhere.

I nodded at Mike and moved on. I didn't feel too sorry for the mark. He'd get to show his girl how hard he'd work to make her happy. And she'd have fun watching her man doing his best to win everything her heart desired. If they didn't spend the money at the peach baskets, they'd just spend it somewhere else. At the end of the day, they'd bring home a bunch of happy memories and a couple prizes.

Even so, I knew I couldn't run a game the way Mike did. I'd filled in at games for a few minutes here and there, but I never hustled the players. I didn't even say much. I couldn't chat with strangers. Mike sure could. He made them feel like he was their best friend. I just took the money and handed over the balls or the darts or whatever the game required.

But in a little while, I was going to get my chance to say anything I wanted. And say it to anyone I felt like picking from the crowd.

I walked a little farther, and treated myself to a slice at

Salvatore's. I didn't even know how much I was getting paid tonight, but I figured it would be decent, especially if I did a great job. Maybe Bob paid out a percentage of the take. That would be awesome. I was sure the booth raked in at least eighty bucks an hour when things were going full speed.

I headed back. My stomach was churning and I ended up tossing away most of the slice. The crowds were definitely heavier now. Mike was working hard when I went past. He had players at all four baskets. *That* kept him busy. He didn't have to do any talking. He didn't really have a chance. He spent most of his time gathering up the balls from the ground. I didn't envy him that part—his back probably ached from all the bending. Better him than me.

Even before I got near Wild Willy's Pier, I could see a thick crowd around the Bozo tank. As I got closer, I heard Malcolm's insane laugh. I guess Bob had given him an earlier shift. Too bad. I'd hoped he'd be gone. I reached the edge of the crowd. Thwunks from missed shots mingled with the occasional clang and splash. A ripple of goose bumps chilled my arms beneath my sleeves. The air had started to cool off. I wondered whether I should have worn a heavier shirt.

I worked my way through the mob, wishing I hadn't eaten any pizza at all. The sauce burned like acid in my throat. *Relax,* I told myself. *You'll be behind a cage. And in makeup. You'll be great.* I wondered how Malcolm would feel when he found out who was going to be working the tank for the best part of the evening.

I had to push my way to the front. "Hey. I'm here, Boss," I said as I reached Bob. "I'm ready to start."

Bob stared at me for a second with no sign of recognition. Then he broke into a smile. "Right—the new kid. Excellent. I was wondering if you'd show up. Glad you came. It's getting busy." He took the money that a man in front of him was waving in his face and handed over three balls. Then he gave me several greasy bills. "Here. You mind getting me a cheeseburger before you start?"

"No problem, Boss."

I rushed across the boardwalk and got Bob his food.

"Thanks," he said, taking the burger from me. "You ready?"

"Yeah, I'm ready." I scanned the crowds pressing in from the sides. Man, there were a lot of people. I glanced over at Malcolm. I guess he wasn't going to get out of the tank until I put on my makeup. No point leaving it empty. But he'd be gone soon enough.

"You know what to do?" Bob asked.

"Absolutely. I've been thinking about it all day. I know I just—"

"Good boy." He bent over and picked up an empty five-gallon bucket that had a damp, dirty towel draped over the side. "Here," he said, thrusting it out toward me.

I grabbed the bucket automatically as it jammed against my chest.

"Just be careful. Watch your head. The first kid I hired last year caught one right in the nose. Probably have to go through the rest of his life looking like a very untalented boxer."

I didn't get it. "Won't the bars protect me?"

Bob gave me a puzzled look. "Not where you're gonna be." He stopped to take another two bucks from the mark, then said, "Just make sure you don't try to collect the balls while someone's throwing."

Collect the balls?

The truth crashed over me like a ten-foot wave. I was such an idiot. How could I have thought he was hiring me to go in the tank? I lowered my head and saw my work spread out in front of me. Baseballs were scattered around the canvas behind the target. There was a puddle by the bottom of the tank that grew larger every time the Bozo plunged into the water. The wood supporting the tank was solid, so there was nowhere for the water to drain. A lot of the balls had rolled to a stop in the puddle. That explained the towel.

"Well, come on," Bob said. "Hustle."

Bloody freakin' crap. I wanted to slam down the bucket and stomp away. But I was trapped by my own big mouth. I'd told him I'd do the job—even bragged about what a dependable worker I was. *The best. Ask anyone.* I'd have to come through. Just for tonight. It couldn't be that tough. I walked behind him and nearly got my head taken off as a huge guy wearing a Dallas Cowboys T-shirt hurled a ball full force.

Nobody noticed my close brush with death.

I dodged out of the way and waited until the Cowboys fan was finished, then dashed forward and scooped up a couple of the balls. I gave them a quick wipe with the towel before I dumped them in the bucket. There were so many balls scattered around, and the players were throwing them so fast, I barely managed to keep up.

As I chased after a ball that had rolled behind the tank, the Bozo's voice tore through the speakers. "Glad I don't have your job. Talk about a pathetic way to earn money."

"Shut up!" I shouted, spinning toward him.

He wasn't even looking at me. Or talking to me. He was pointing at a guy in the crowd wearing a bright-orange Highway Department vest. I guess the guy had just gotten off work.

"Real hard job, right? You the genius who holds the sign that says *Stop?* Where'd you go to learn that trade? Moron school?"

The highway guy threw eighteen balls before he dunked Malcolm. I was rooting for the mark the whole time.

Not that I had much of a chance to think. I was too busy ducking, dashing, stooping, and scooping. And wiping. The water in the puddles was unbelievably gross. People had all sorts of crap on their hands when they grabbed the balls. The towel looked like something that had been used to diaper a baby gorilla. That wasn't the worst part. My knees hurt from hitting them on the boardwalk. My back hurt from all the bending. My clothes were wet from getting splashed and from kneeling in puddles. And my pride had been crushed past any hope of recovery. Someone I knew was bound to spot me sooner or later.

On top of everything else that made this a nightmare, there was no safe place to hide. Most of the balls hit the canvas and dropped. But there were plenty of wild throws. Once in a while someone got real angry and hurled a shot right at the cage. The Bozo was safe behind the bars. I wasn't. There was no way to know how the ball would bounce. It was like being caught inside a giant pinball machine.

Those damn bars. They made all the difference. I was on the outside, trying not to get killed, while that freak Malcolm was on the inside, where I belonged.

At one point I heard someone shout, "Hey, look at Chad."

I glanced over and saw Anthony with a couple of his friends. None of them was close to being able to walk a straight line. Malcolm ignored him. I'd noticed he didn't pick any vics who were too far gone. I ignored Anthony, too. Unfortunately, he didn't ignore me. "Wow, Bozo's ball boy," he said. "Ballzo!" He cackled at his great wit. "Yeah, Ballzo."

They moved on, and all I could do was hope that he was so stoned he'd forget the nickname before he had a chance to spread it around. I couldn't go through the rest of high school as Ballzo. I'd be getting into fights every day.

All in all, it was absolutely the most awful two hours I'd ever spent in my life, not counting the time when I was seven and came down with a stomach virus in the middle of a class trip to the Philadelphia Zoo. Maybe this was worse. Malcolm worked the crowd the whole time, never letting up. He had players coming one right after another. I didn't get any chance to rest. The two times Bob sent me for food, I had to run both ways so I wouldn't fall too far behind. The only thing that saved me from dying was that it was still early in the season. The action started to drop off around nine. If I'd had to go much longer, I never would have made it out of there alive.

"You can knock off now if you want, kid," Bob said when the pace had slowed enough so he could handle it.

I nodded, too tired to even talk.

Malcolm still didn't let up. "Wow. I had no idea lizards could walk so well on two legs," he called to a mark.

Bob reached into his change apron and pulled out a thick bundle of cash. "Let's see. You worked two hours. Minus the rental fee for the bucket and the towel. And union dues, of course."

"What?"

"Relax, kid. I'm just playing with your mind." He riffled the money with his thumb, then pulled off a couple bills and jammed them in the pocket of my pants.

"Thanks."

"See you tomorrow, same time?" He turned away from me to do business with Malcolm's latest vic.

I tried to think of the best way to tell him I was quitting.

Bob handed the player three balls, glanced back at me, and said, "I have to admit, you told the truth. You're a hard worker. Good to know I can count on you." He slapped me on the back, then gave me a shove. "Go on. Run around. Have fun. Go do whatever it is you kids do these days."

I staggered away, propelled by his shove. My pants were soaked all the way up to my knees, and my socks were so wet they squished with each step. All the pains merged into one giant ache. I managed to drag myself a couple blocks. Then I dropped onto a bench that faced out toward the water. All around me, the lights kept flashing, the rides kept running, the people kept walking and playing and spending. But my mind had nearly shut down. Numb and exhausted, I reached into my pocket and pulled out the money, wondering how badly Bob had ripped me off.

THE FIRST BILL WAS A TEN. THE SECOND WAS A TWENTY. BOTH were stained with mustard, but I didn't care. Even the little piece of dried sauerkraut didn't bother me. Thirty dollars for two hours of work. I stared at the bills for a moment. Then I remembered where I was and jammed the money deep into my pants pocket. Anybody flashing around cash was asking for trouble. You never knew who was in the crowd. It just took one person who was desperate enough, or wasted enough, and someone would get hurt.

As if I wasn't already hurting. I got up and staggered toward home. When I reached the ramp for my block, I plopped down on another bench and put my feet up on the railing. I took a deep breath of the night air, heavy with the scent of salt and kelp. Man, it felt good to sit back. At least it did until somebody threw a choke hold around my neck.

I panicked as the arm slipped under my chin and tightened against my throat, pinning my back to the bench. "You know what I want," my attacker whispered, his hot breath washing across my ear. The grip grew tighter, threatening to crush my windpipe. "I want your priceless collection of dirty socks."

I relaxed as I recognized Jason's voice. He released my neck and plopped down next to me.

"I thought you'd gone home to die," I said.

He shook his head. "I'm great. All I needed was some sleep. Now, you, on the other hand, look like someone who's not going to be around for long. What'd you do, ride the coasters all night?"

"No such luck." I told him about my evening's work.

After I was done, all he said was, "Wow, thirty bucks. Good deal. Run the numbers, man. You can make over two hundred a week, if he keeps paying you that much. Of course, maybe part of that was like a first-day bonus. Even so, looks like you found a gold mine. Or a golden goose. Or whatever."

I shook my head. "No way. I can't do it."

"California," Jason said. "Close your eyes and imagine the beach. Imagine a place where it never snows. You know how many colleges there are near there? And that means lots of college girls. You gotta stick with it."

"Can't," I said. It was more than the aches and pains. It killed me to spend all that time listening to Malcolm, watching him work and knowing he wasn't going to invite me to trade places. *Come on, Chad, hop right in. The water's fine.* Yeah, right.

"Santa Monica," Jason said. "There's a pier. Rides. Games. Food. They have tournaments all the time. I can make big money out there. We'll buy an arcade with my volleyball winnings."

"Home," I said, getting up from the bench. "It has a bed, blankets, and a pillow. No college girls, but nothing's perfect." I staggered a couple steps and tried not to groan. My muscles were already growing stiff.

"Wow, you really are hurting," Jason said. "Let me

help." He bent down, threw an arm around my back, and lifted me onto his shoulder.

"Knock it off!" I yelled as the world turned upside down. "I can walk."

I could feel Jason shake his head. "Nope. What are friends for?" He jogged toward the ramp. "I can't let you down."

Naturally, people stared at us as we left the boardwalk. I hated that. They probably thought I was wasted. At least they didn't stare too long or too hard. There was enough other stuff going on to catch their attention. Besides, people got carried off the boardwalk all the time.

Jason finally put me down after he'd lugged me a block. I looked carefully at his face. I was worried he'd pass out again. I weighed more than the boxes we'd carried this afternoon. As far as I could tell, he seemed fine. I guess whatever was wrong with him, it was over.

"Hey, you're bleeding," Jason said. He pointed to my back.

"What?" I remembered getting banged and bruised, but not cut. "Where?" There didn't seem to be any sharp pains mixed in with the aches.

Jason leaned over and took a closer look. "No, wait." I felt his finger press against my back. Then he rubbed his finger against his thumb. "Oh, yuck. It's ketchup. What were you doing? Rolling on the boardwalk?"

I thought about the shove Bob had given me. "Just about." I left it at that and concentrated on hauling my sore body the remaining two and a half blocks.

"So," Jason asked when we reached my house, "you're going to keep working there, aren't you?"

The thought made me shudder. "I don't think so." But he was right about one thing. The money was great. And maybe I could talk Bob into giving me a chance in the tank. Besides, I thought, as I pushed down a twinge of guilt that threatened to enter the picture, if it was only two hours a night, it really didn't count as a job. So I wasn't going behind Mom's back.

"Say yes, man," Jason urged.

"I don't know. Maybe." The feel of the money came back to me. It was washed away as a jolt of pain ran through my elbow where I'd gotten clipped by a wild throw. "No. Definitely not. I'm done with it."

"That's what I like about you, Chad. Once you make up your mind, you never change it—at least, not more than five or ten times a second."

"No. I've made up my mind for sure. I quit."

"And I suppose that's your final answer?"

"Yeah." I started up the walkway to the porch.

"Careful," Jason said. "Quitting can become a habit."

Those words felt like a knife in my back. I spun around to face him. "You think I don't know that?" I shouted. "You think I need a lecture? Give me a break, okay?" Nobody could tell me anything I didn't know about quitting. I was the son of a world-champion quitter. And I sure didn't need anyone to remind me of that.

Jason took a step back. "Sorry. I didn't mean it that way."

"I'm not like my dad," I said. I remembered how he'd always wait until dinner to drop the news. *I quit that job today, Annie. Just didn't work out.* He'd list all the reasons, and Mom would sit, not saying anything, her face marked by sadness and worry as she slowly pulled her napkin apart. Then he'd eat his food like everything was just fine, and Mom would let her meal go untouched.

"Of course not," Jason said.

I clenched my teeth, afraid that if I kept talking I'd say something rotten. And that would be stupid. The last thing I needed was to lose my best friend right at the start of summer.

"Hey, I hear the water's supposed to warm up tomorrow," Jason said. "How about we hit the beach?"

I nodded and took a long, slow breath, trying to push the anger and frustration deep down where they wouldn't do any harm. "Sounds like a plan." I dragged my aching bones inside.

I never thought a bed could feel so good. Especially not a convertible. But the instant my body touched the mattress, I was out. If I had dreams, I didn't even remember them. The world just switched off until Mom shook my shoulder.

"Going to sleep the whole day away?" she asked.

I squinted at the clock. Ten thirty. I guess Mom had stopped by between breakfast and lunch. "Maybe." I put my head back down.

"You shouldn't waste the summer sleeping," she said.

"How should I waste it, then?"

"Do things. Make new friends. Read some good books. Enjoy yourself."

"Okay. I'll do that after breakfast." I pushed my face deeper into the pillow.

Mom yanked the pillow out from under me and stripped off the pillowcase, which she tossed into a basket full of dirty clothes at the foot of the couch. "Don't forget to do the wash."

"That sounds enjoyable. Maybe I'll make some new friends in the Laundromat."

She bent over and gave me a kiss on the top of the head. "I'll see you after work."

"Bye."

I dozed for a while longer, putting off the moment when I'd actually find out what it felt like to move.

A knock on the door woke me. I rolled off the couch and got to my feet. Everything ached. I felt like I'd been beaten up by professional thugs. Or talented amateurs.

I managed to cross the room. On the other side of the door was the last person I wanted to see.

"Rent," Malcolm said, handing me an envelope. He switched into a shaky old-lady voice. "Please don't send me out into the cold, Mr. Landlord."

I walked over to the kitchen counter and wrote out a receipt, then went back and shoved it at him.

"You worked hard last night," he said.

I didn't bother to answer. He was such a total jerk.

He switched to a funny voice, wiggling his eyebrows and flicking an imaginary cigar. "Hey, it's a dirty job, but somebody's got to do it."

I didn't laugh. No way I was going to be his audience. I wasn't some mark at the Bozo tank.

"Well, have a nice day." He headed off.

After he left, I took a long, hot shower, ate, then carried the overloaded basket down the street to the Laundromat. At least it wasn't far. I didn't make any new friends. But I washed and dried the clothes. Right after I got home, I put on my bathing suit and called Jason. Then I turned the TV up loud to drown out the stupid voice that kept looping through my mind. . . . *It's a dirty job, but somebody's got to do it.* . . . Not me. Not that job. I couldn't do it. I wanted to quit, but I didn't want to be a quitter. There had to be another way out.

15

WHEN JASON SHOWED UP, I SCANNED HIS FACE FOR ANY SIGN that he was angry about the way I'd shouted at him last night. Not a hint. Which made me feel even more guilty. "Hey, sorry about . . . you know . . ."

"No sweat, *amigo*," Jason said. "You recovered from your labors?"

"Still hurting," I said. I almost added, *Carry me*. But I kept my mouth shut because I knew Jason would actually do it. I grabbed a towel and we headed out, turning the corner and joining the stream of people who flowed toward the water all day.

It's funny listening to tourists when they see the beach for the first time. They'll say stuff like *Oh, good lord, where's the water?* There's a quarter mile of hot sand between the boardwalk and the ocean—even more at low tide. You can't really tell what's ahead until you cross under the boardwalk. Then, it's like gazing over vast empty stretches of desert. I think the town should buy a couple of camels, just for the effect.

People spill out of the motels carrying a ton and a half of stuff—beach mats, chairs, umbrellas, boogie boards, sand buckets, books, coolers, Frisbees, kites, radios, and dozens of other essential items. They can't wait to hit the water or fry themselves in the sun.

When you're barefoot, on hot sand, with both arms loaded, a quarter mile is a long, long way to trek.

Jason and I knew better, of course. I had a towel on my shoulder and sandals on my feet. So did he. We passed under the boardwalk, then back into the sunshine.

"There's Mike and Corey," Jason said, pointing out the two of them over to our left as we got close to the surf. We joined them and spread out our towels. Mike was wearing a pair of cutoffs and his favorite beach toy—mirrored sunglasses. Corey wore knee-length shorts, a T-shirt, a hat, and about a half gallon of sunscreen. He smelled like a coconut.

"Time off?" I asked Mike.

He nodded. "Just till four. Then I'm on till closing. What's up?"

"Chad got a job," Jason said. He kicked off his sandals and dropped down on his towel. "He's working at the dunk tank."

"Sounds cool," Corey said.

"It was awful." I listed some of the details, which made me even less eager to go back. But I wasn't going to quit after only one day. "It's got to be the worst job in the world."

"Uh-uh," Corey said. "There are lots worse. I had an uncle who was a tester for insect repellent. They'd spray his arms with different formulas and then he'd stick them in a tank full of mosquitoes."

"That's nothing," Jason said. "Back in New York, a couple of the older kids I knew made money selling their blood. You're only supposed to sell some every two weeks, and you're not supposed to sell it at all if you're underage, but they'd go to a bunch of different places."

"Yuck," Mike said. "But that's not a job, is it? I mean, you don't do it all day long."

"Maybe, but it's still pretty rough by the third or fourth pint," Jason said.

"How about fixing clogged toilets?" Corey asked. "That can't be fun."

"That's not so bad," Mike told him. "It's not like you do it with your bare hands. My neighbor's a plumber. He makes good money. Now, sitting in an office somewhere . . . the same place all day every day—that's got to suck."

"Depends what you do," Corey said. "I can spend the whole day on my computer. No problem."

"Basically, working sucks," Mike said. "That's why I'm joining the army. You know exactly what's going to happen, and they won't fire you if business gets slow. No matter what, you get your check and you get your meals." He plopped back on his towel. I couldn't see his eyes behind the sunglasses, but I could tell from the way his head moved that he was watching every girl who walked by. Even without the glasses, the girls wouldn't have noticed what he was doing because they were all too busy checking out Jason.

"Agreed," Corey said. "Working sucks."

I hoped they were wrong. Two more years of school, and then I'd be doing some kind of work. Maybe I'd really get to own an arcade. Or maybe I'd be the guy sticking his arm in a cloud of mosquitoes. I didn't have a clue where I'd end up. It didn't seem like I had any control over that right now. Or maybe ever. And even after all these years of school, I hadn't found anything I thought I'd be good at. Until now.

Jason stood up and stretched. "Swim?" he asked.

"Go ahead. I'll be there in a bit."

He jogged to the edge of the water and stuck a toe into the surf as it lapped toward him. After a moment he backed up a couple steps, then ran straight ahead, letting out a shout when the water reached his waist. He leaped up and dove under a wave as it broke in front of him.

"He never stops," Corey said.

"Why don't you join him?" I asked. The whole time I'd known Corey, I hadn't ever seen him go into the water. He claimed he was allergic to salt.

"No, thanks." He grabbed his bottle of sunscreen and started applying another layer.

I glanced at Wild Willy's Pier, which jutted toward the ocean on our right. The Green Tarantula, one of the largest inverted coasters in the East, towered over the water. I loved watching the cars when they went through the first loop, throwing the riders' feet straight up as the track shot past under their heads. Seconds later, they blew through a double corkscrew. We were too far away to hear the screams.

"What do you think it would cost to build a dunk tank?" I asked.

"Two or three hundred, at least," Mike said. "Lumber's pretty expensive, but you could use scrap iron for the bars."

"Maybe another eighty for cheap speakers and a microphone," Corey said. "Wait, you'd need an amplifier, too. Make it one twenty."

"That's still not too bad." I imagined having my own tank on the boardwalk, near a busy pier or next to one of the major coasters. I'd hire my friends to work the front. Pay them good money. I'd work the tank, of course. Maybe put the earnings into building a second tank. Train some other Bozos. Build up a whole business.

"Don't forget, you need a place to put it," Mike told me. "Rent's not cheap around here. My boss always complains about that when he's explaining why I can't get a raise. You gotta pay for water and electricity, of course."

"And there's insurance," Corey said. "Workmen's comp, taxes, Social Security. There's probably some sort of licensing fee from the township. Maybe you even have to a post a liability bond."

Man, I didn't know the first thing about that kind of stuff. How did anyone ever start a business when there was so much nonsense to deal with? I sighed and turned my attention back to the ocean.

I watched Jason for a while, then went to join him. I didn't like to dive in. I waded, standing on my toes each time a swell threatened to reach a dry part of my body. But after getting smacked with a couple high waves, I was as wet as Jason.

"Feels great," he said.

He was right. I think there's something in salt water that can heal just about anything. My muscles felt better. All of me felt better.

Jason pointed toward the beach. "People dream all year of a week at the shore. And we live here."

"Pretty good deal," I said. I stood for a while, letting the motion of the water bury my feet beneath the sand. I floated and I swam a bit, then climbed out and plopped down on my towel. But something caught my attention.

A large group of guys was tossing around a couple Frisbees near the water off to our left. "Hey," I asked, sitting up, "speaking of biting insects, isn't that Stinger?"

Mike turned his head briefly away from two girls passing near us in bikinis. "Sure is."

I didn't recognize the other guys with Stinger. But I had a suspicion who they might be, and with that suspicion came a thought that made me grin. If I was right, I was facing an irresistible opportunity.

"What are you so happy about?" Jason asked as he came up from the water. He ran both hands through his hair, pushing off a shower of drops.

"The chance of a lifetime," I said. "I'll be back." I jogged over to say hi to Stinger. He'd just graduated, and was sort of a school hero. I knew him from study hall and we got along okay. About half the guys in his group wore orange T-shirts with CAMP SIZZLE printed in black letters on the back. Red flames burst from the first letter of each word, and the whole name was underlined with a lightning bolt.

"Hey, Stinger," I said when he spotted me. "How's it going?"

"Hey, Chad." He nodded. "It's going good. You?"

"Can't complain. You here for a while?"

"Just till tonight. Came over with some of the guys from camp. Whatcha been doing?" He leaped up and grabbed a Frisbee as it passed overhead.

"Working on the boardwalk. At a dunk tank."

"Sounds like fun," he said as he flicked the Frisbee to one of his friends who was standing knee-deep in the water.

"It keeps me hustling. Stop by before you leave. It's right in front of Wild Willy's. I'll be there any time after seven."

Stinger nodded. "I'll swing by if I get a chance."

"Great." I headed to my towel.

"What was that all about?" Jason asked when I got back.

"Oh, I just thought Malcolm might get a kick out of meeting Stinger and his friends."

"Oh, man," Jason said, shaking his head. "You're rotten. Truly rotten."

"You think so?"

"Definitely."

"Thanks." I lay back and let the sun warm my smiling face. There was no question in my mind anymore. I knew for sure I was going back to the dunk tank. No way I'd miss it. Stinger could probably hit the target with his eyes closed. Tonight was going to be interesting.

16

"I'M HERE," I TOLD BOB WHEN I GOT TO THE TANK THAT evening. It was only six forty. I wanted to make sure I didn't miss Stinger.

"Good to see you. I kind of figured you wouldn't be back. Half the kids I hire quit after the first day. Or sooner. Especially the kid who got hit on the nose. He pretty much quit right then." Bob waved the remains of a stick of cotton candy in the general direction of the bucket. "You might as well get to work."

It was just as awful as it had been the night before. And even more dangerous. I nearly got nailed a couple times because I kept searching the crowd. But tonight I didn't care about the filth or the pain or the danger. Whatever I had to deal with, it would all be worthwhile. As long as Stinger came.

About half an hour after I got there, I caught a couple flashes of orange heading toward the tank. It was Stinger, and he wasn't alone. There were nine or ten guys with him. This was perfect. More than perfect.

Earlier, I'd kicked one of the balls so it rolled behind the tank. Now I rushed over to grab it, just as Malcolm got dunked.

"Hey," I said, loudly enough to get his attention as he

climbed out of the water. I had to hurry before he chose another mark.

"What?"

"See that kid in the orange T-shirt? The one with the crew cut."

"Yeah, I see him."

"I know him from school. He used to pick on me all the time."

"You want to get even?" Malcolm asked.

"Yeah, I want to get even," I said. That was sure true. I couldn't help grinning in anticipation. Man, was I about to get even. Big time. "Think you can show him what it's like to get picked on?"

"No problem." Malcolm looked over at Stinger. I could almost hear his Bozo brain working, searching for the perfect hook to sink into his victim so he could drag him into the game. I wondered what he'd pick. Stinger was tall and thin. He looked kind of awkward when he walked. And his hair was in a buzz cut. I figured Malcolm could start out using any of those things.

But the Bozo homed in on something else. "Well, what do we have here?" he asked. He let the question hang in the air just long enough to get everyone's attention, then supplied an answer. "It's a traveling herd of oranges."

The crowd shifted as everyone inched away from Stinger and his pals.

"My mistake," Malcolm said. "You're such a close bunch, you must be bananas." He let out a Bozo howl to punctuate the joke. The crowd started laughing.

I watched Stinger's face. He was about the calmest guy I knew. Pressure meant nothing to him. He was used to being shouted at. He'd been called far worse names than anything Malcolm would say in public. There was a chance he'd just shake off the comments and walk away. *Come on, I thought, go for it.*

"Yes!" I said as Stinger smiled that calm, deadly smile and strolled over to Bob.

"Oh, no," Malcolm said. "One of them got loose. Save me!" He glanced frantically from side to side in the tank, as if his life was in danger.

Stinger took the three balls with his right hand and passed one of them to his left. He tossed the ball up about a foot and let it fall back into his waiting fingers. Then he did it again.

"It's a baseball," Malcolm said. "What's wrong? Never seen one before? Stop playing catch with yourself and throw the stupid thing."

That's exactly what Stinger did. His first throw nailed the target dead center with a deafening clang, plunging Malcolm into the water.

Malcolm climbed back on the seat and leaned over to say something into the microphone. But before he had a chance to speak, Stinger, using the same beautifully smooth motion, nailed the target a second time.

And then he nailed it a third time.

While I gathered up the three balls, Stinger paid Bob another two bucks. Behind him, his buddies cheered and whistled. And they lined up for their turns. The crowd drew closer, suddenly sensing that this time the vic was inside the cage.

Stinger threw another three pitches, just as perfectly as he'd done from the mound at Pinecrest High, where he'd led the Pine Devils to an undefeated season with his eighty-five-mile-per-hour fastball. He was off to college in the fall on a full scholarship. But first he'd stopped at Camp Sizzle, a local pitching camp where the best of the best get fine-tuned. Anyone who'd lived around here for long knew about the camp. Malcolm, on the other hand, had no clue what he'd just unleashed.

I caught sight of Jason in the crowd, far over to the right. He shook his head and mouthed the words, "You're bad."

Yeah, I was bad. And I loved it. Stinger hurled three more balls, all dead on target, and then stepped aside to let one of the other star pitchers have a turn.

Malcolm didn't even get a chance to open his mouth. Nearly every single throw plunged him into the water. The crowd loved it, too. A couple times I saw money passing hands. People were actually betting on the pitchers.

"Tough night," Bob said when I delivered a bucketful of balls.

I shrugged. "It happens."

Once or twice, when I got close to the cage, I looked at Malcolm and said, "Hey, it's a dirty job, but somebody's got to do it."

My work was easy. The players had to wait between throws while Malcolm crawled back onto the ledge. I didn't have any trouble keeping up, especially since Malcolm got slower and slower.

Now we're even, I thought as the last member of Stinger's group took his turn. Back in January I'd been over at Corey's house when he was washing his cat. Corey's got bad allergies, and the doctor suggested either getting rid of the cat or at least giving it a bath every couple weeks. Until now I'd never seen anything sadder climbing out of the water than Corey's cat. But Malcolm was looking pretty pathetic. And pretty exhausted. The effort of hauling himself back on that ledge so many times had to be tiring. Even so, I figured he'd gotten off pretty easily.

But it wasn't over.

Stinger and the rest of the pitchers did the one thing guys are best at—they made a game of it. They lined up again and each player took a turn. Whoever missed had to drop out. Then the rest of the pitchers went for another round.

Malcolm spent more time in the water than on the ledge.

Eventually, it got down to Stinger and two other guys. Nobody missed for a while. It seemed like it would never end. Then, finally, the other two guys missed, one right after the other.

Enough, I thought as Stinger threw his final ball. He raised his hands in victory, then waved at me and walked through the cheering fans, along with his friends from Camp Sizzle.

A large part of the crowd drifted away now that the show was over. Bob tapped his watch to let me know it was nine o'clock. Oh, man—I never expected the whole thing would last that long.

17

"You can knock off," Bob said as he pulled out his wad of cash. He frowned as if he was doing some sort of calculation. "Sorry it's not more. Bad night for all of us. Guess my uncle's going to have to wait a little longer for that heart operation we've been saving up for."

"What?"

"Just playing with your mind," Bob said, grinning at me with teeth that weren't entirely free of hot-dog relish. "Here, take this." He handed me two bills.

"Thanks." I joined Jason over at the far right edge of the crowd.

"Man," he said. "That was brutal. I wouldn't have stayed in there, would you?"

"I don't know." I wondered what I would have done if I'd been in Malcolm's place. It would be easy to leave the tank, I guess. Nobody would know who I was. But it would still feel like quitting. On the other hand, what's the point in letting yourself get destroyed? It was only a job. Or was that the sort of excuse that quitters always used? *I quit that job today. Just didn't work out.*

I watched Malcolm crawl onto the ledge and, for the first time in nearly two hours, open his mouth. "Hey, how about that?" He paused and scanned the crowd. "Yeah, how about that. . . . That was really something. . . ."

I wondered whether he had anything left. He must have gone into the water a couple hundred times. He'd sat there knowing that almost every throw was going to send him plunging. It had to be kind of like standing in front of a firing squad. Maybe he was afraid the whole boardwalk was loaded with talented pitchers tonight.

The remaining crowd started to drift off.

"Guess I got dunked, huh?"

A couple people laughed.

"What are you laughing at, farm boy?" Malcolm called to a skinny guy wearing overalls and a white T-shirt. His voice didn't have its usual harsh edge. "You take a wrong turn with your tractor?"

The guy threw three balls and missed three times. Then he shrugged and started to walk away.

I waited to see whether Malcolm would get him to try again. He couldn't allow the mark to escape that easily.

"Let's go," Jason said. "I'm tired of watching him take the plunge."

"Just a minute."

"Come on. Let's get some pizza. I practiced for three hours this afternoon. I'm starving." He turned and headed north.

"Okay," I said as I caught up with him. "But let's go to Salvatore's."

"That's where I was going," Jason said.

I pointed south. "Salvatore's is that way."

Jason looked around for a second, then nodded. "Yeah.

Right." He turned and we headed back past the dunk tank. I wasn't surprised at his mistake. The boardwalk is so long, and so crowded with games and shops, that almost everyone gets confused once in a while—even people who live here.

Behind us, I could hear Malcolm saying something about cows and overalls. I couldn't tell if the guy took the bait. Pretty soon the sound of the rides and the crowds drowned out anything from the Bozo tank.

"How about Stinger," I said. "Ever see anything like that?"

Jason shook his head. "Not in this lifetime. Speaking of which, have you figured out how to keep Malcolm from killing you?"

"What's he going to do? It's part of the job. Just one of the risks he has to take. He might have run into Stinger even without my help. Right?"

"Maybe," Jason said. "But I wouldn't want to try to convince him of that."

"Forget about it." I checked the money Bob had given me. A five and a ten. "My treat," I told Jason. When we got to Salvatore's, I ordered a whole pie. I splurged for a large bottle of soda, too. One of the three-liter deals.

"You guys win the lottery?" Salvatore called from behind the counter when the waitress brought us the pie.

"Chad's been working hard," Jason called back.

"Or hardly working," Salvatore joked, almost as if it was a reflex.

An ache in my side told me Jason was right. I'd been working hard. In a way it felt good, like after a rough game of football with the guys. I'd earned the pains. But this was better than a hard day of sports. I had money in my pocket. I'd been paid for every ounce of agony. My good feeling slipped away when I thought about Malcolm. If I closed my eyes, I could see him plunging into the water, over and over. It was like one of those movies where people live through the same thing endlessly until they figure out how to get it right.

"So you going back tomorrow?" Jason asked.

I took a small bite from the tip of my slice. It was just hot enough to burn the top of my mouth. I sucked in air to cool the cheese, then managed to chew without searing too much flesh. "I don't know. The work really rots. But the money's great." That was the worst part—I didn't know what I wanted to do. I had reasons for quitting. I had reasons for not quitting. Why did everything have to be so complicated?

"As long as your mom doesn't find out."

"She wouldn't care," I said. "It's not like a real job. I mean, it's just a couple hours a day. It's no different from running errands for an hour or two. I'm just running a whole bunch of short errands in a very small place. I don't think she'd have a problem with that."

"Maybe you should ask her."

"Nope, I don't have to. I'm sure she wouldn't mind." I didn't have any doubts about that. Besides, the best way to avoid getting turned down was to avoid asking.

We finished our pizza, then walked to the south end of the boardwalk, where we watched a couple drunks get tattoos.

"Man, I'll bet he's starting to wish his girlfriend had a shorter name," Jason whispered to me as the tattoo artist sketched out a heart and *Annabella* in ballpoint pen on this guy's chest. His buddy, who'd already gotten a dagger on his left shoulder, was slumped back, half passed out in one of the chairs along the side wall.

"Sure hope Annabella doesn't dump him," I said.

Jason nodded. "Yeah, when it comes to tattoos, there aren't any do-overs."

"Are there ever?" I asked. Each choice people made in life seemed to add a couple dots of ink to the picture.

Jason just shrugged.

By the time we headed home, everything was winding down. Two girls were closing up the Cat-a-Pult. They stopped to watch Jason as we went past. *Give it up,* I told myself. It was like that kid's song about Clementine. She was lost and gone forever.

The dunk tank sat dark and empty in the shadows. A scattering of crumbs, peanut shells, and ketchup splats showed where Bob had been standing. I walked up to the tank and looked inside, wondering what it felt like to plunge into the water. Wondering even more how it would feel to lean into that microphone and let loose, free to say anything to anyone.

The bars creaked and shifted beneath my hand. "Hey, it's not locked up." This was too good a chance to miss. The crowds might be gone, but I could at least see what it felt like from the inside. I swung open the gate.

"Dude, you're the only guy on the planet who would break *into* a cage," Jason said.

"I guess I'm just special. Mind if I practice on you?" I asked. I knew I could do a lot better than Malcolm's stupid blond jokes.

"Go right ahead."

"Cool." It would only be fair, after all the times I'd let Jason practice volleyball with me. I stuck one leg through the opening and over the ledge. As I got ready to swing my other leg inside, a blinding light struck me in the eyes.

"All right, you, what's going on here?"

I squinted past the beam, barely making out two figures standing side by side.

"It's okay, I work here," I said. That was a break. There was no way I could get in trouble.

"I don't see any work being done." The light dropped lower, playing over my chest and hands, allowing me to open my eyes wider than a squint. For a moment, all I could see was a large yellow blotch. Then it faded, revealing who I was facing. Oh, crap—it was the same two cops who'd almost busted me the other day.

"We just closed up. I work here, for Bob. He runs it. I was checking to make sure the water level was okay for to-morrow." I knew they didn't care whether I belonged there or not. They just wanted to hassle me.

Officer Costas waved the flashlight. "Get over here."

I swung my leg back out. Officer Manetti pulled a pad from his belt and asked for our names. Officer Costas stared at me, and then at Jason. "It's not worth our time to bring you punks in," he said.

"Move along," Officer Manetti said.

"Thanks," Jason said.

Before I could take a step, Officer Costas tapped the bars of the Bozo tank with his flashlight. "If you really want to spend time in a cage, I can arrange it." I guess it was sup-posed to be a joke, but he didn't laugh. Neither did I.

"I hate them," I muttered as I slunk off with Jason.

"They're just doing their job," Jason said.

"I don't care. I still hate them. That's twice this week. I haven't done a damn thing, and they act like I'm some kind of criminal." I kicked the back of a bench hard enough to send a jolt through my ankle.

We left the boardwalk at Fifteenth Street and headed toward Sea Crest.

"What's up for tomorrow?" I asked Jason when we reached my house.

"Practice. All day. Need to get ready for the tournament."

"Maybe I'll come watch," I said.

"Sure. . . . See ya later." Jason waved and jogged off toward his house. I headed down the walkway to my front door.

A motion on the outside stairs caught my eye. Malcolm rose up from the bottom step and walked toward me.

He was angry. No mistake. And this time, I didn't think he was acting.

18

"You set me up," Malcolm said. He stepped so close I could feel his breath on my face.

"Duh." That's not what I'd wanted to say. I'd wanted to apologize. But those words wouldn't come.

His right hand shot out and grabbed my shirt. In the streetlight his eyes seemed to reflect fire. He pushed me against the wall of the house. I could feel the siding dig into my back.

"You worthless little piece of crap," he said.

I kept my mouth shut as the nature of the situation sunk in. I could get hurt.

"It's hard enough out there." His fist clenched and twisted, drawing the shirt tight against my shoulders. "It's hard enough without you making it worse. You understand?"

"Yeah."

He thrust his face closer to mine. "If you ever—" He stopped in midthreat, let go of my shirt, and backed off. The muscles in his neck flexed as he clenched his jaw. I could tell that one part of him was dying to let loose and kick the living crap out of me. But another part was forcing him to hold off.

It was just a joke. I wanted to tell him that, even if it was a lie. This was never just a joke. This was payback. And I'd loved it, at first. But I was afraid to open my mouth. I figured anything I said could send him over the edge.

"Stay away from me." He took another step back.

I nodded.

"And from the job." He turned and moved quickly, almost silently, up the stairs, leaving me to wonder whether I'd just been fired.

"Great," I muttered as I went inside. Mom was asleep. No light showed through the gap at the bottom of her door. Overhead I heard muted steps, as if Malcolm didn't even want the sound of his existence to share any space with me.

I got in bed, closed my eyes, and added up my life, bouncing around through a jumble of wins and losses. I had a mom who worked so hard at taking care of me that I never saw her. Forget my dad. He wasn't even in the picture. I had a couple good friends. That was worth a lot. I had a job that wasn't really a job. A job I hated and had maybe just lost. I had a home near the ocean. Thousands of people would have loved to live here. I had two more years of school ahead of me, assuming I didn't get kicked out, and then a giant sucking vacuum of a question mark.

I lay in bed, listening to the sounds of passing cars and, every now and then, rowdy groups of students staggering between parties, laughing and shouting in the night. My thoughts turned to my darkest fantasy, my deepest hope. Maybe my mom had just once in her life done something wrong. Maybe, just once, she'd cheated on my dad. Someday she'd tell me about him. Tell me about the man whose son I really was. Not the drifter who'd filled her heart with dreams and left her to pay the bills. I pushed those guilty hopes aside.

I still hadn't slept when the first red rays bled through the edges of the curtains. Feeling half-dead, I got up and went to the fridge. I could at least give Mom a small break. Trying not to clatter any pans, I cooked breakfast.

"Well, you're up early," Mom said as she stepped out of the bedroom twenty minutes later. She sniffed the air. "Bacon?"

"And pancakes." I'd made a bit of a mess, but there'd be lots of time to clean it up. I didn't have any plans for the day, except pick up some odd jobs and watch Jason play volleyball later.

She gave me a quick kiss on the forehead. "Thanks."

"You know, you don't have to work so hard," I said as I slid a pancake onto a plate and handed it to her. "If you weren't going to school, you could get a better job right now." I realized she didn't even need to change jobs. Without school in the way, she could make more at the diner by working a later shift.

Mom sighed and took her plate over to the table. "It'll be a lot easier soon," she said. "Once I get my certificate."

"Right." I wondered what would really happen. Maybe there'd be another degree or certificate or training program, and then another. And jobs with longer and longer hours. Maybe it wouldn't ever end. "Corey's dad works so much, he's never home," I said as I joined her at the table.

Mom didn't say anything.

"What good is the money?"

"Chad, you just don't understand." She reached out and put her hand on my arm. "You don't know what poor is. You have no idea. And I pray every night that you never find out. Poor isn't walking around with five dollars and old sneakers. Poor is walking around hungry, wanting to buy food and knowing you can't because you owe money to every store in town. Poor is when you got no idea if you're going to have a place to sleep tomorrow. Whatever it takes, whatever I have to do, I'm not going to let you go through what I did." Her fingers tightened on my arm.

Oh, man—I was sick of fighting the ghosts of her past. I yanked free from her grip. "I can work, Mom. Don't you understand? I *want* to. Let me take some of the load away." If it wasn't for me, there wouldn't even be a load.

"We'll talk about it later," she said, getting up from the table. "Thanks for the pancakes. They were a nice treat." She hurried out the door.

I finished my food and went back to bed, but I couldn't sleep. So I cleaned up the mess from breakfast, then dragged out the vacuum and did the floors. I realized I was making a lot of noise for this early in the morning. Oh, well. Malcolm would just have to cope.

After doing every chore I could think of around the house, I headed to the boardwalk. It was still early—not even seven yet. This was the most dangerous time to be out. People think places are more dangerous at night. But I'd take my chances at three in the morning. At least then you had a shot at avoiding trouble. Right now the boardwalk was filled with joggers and bike riders. They only allowed bikes out here early in the day.

The local bike riders weren't a problem. But any joker with a couple bucks could rent wheels. That meant the boardwalk was loaded with speeding, wobbling, sightseeing vacationers who were so busy staring at stuff in the sky or on the horizon, they ran into anything that didn't dodge in time. *Look, Helen! A bird!* Crash . . . *Look at those kites, Wayne.* Smash . . . *Lookee there, boys, a sailboat. See it?* Wham . . .

To make things worse, people could also rent skates. Toss that into the mix and a peaceful walk became as challenging as crossing a superhighway in a hailstorm.

On the other hand, morning was a great time to pick up odd jobs. The shop owners were getting ready for the day ahead. A guy who suddenly realized he needed a part for his snow-cone machine or a new tape for his cash register would be real happy to see me coming by.

I stayed near the railing as I walked. That was the safest spot. People zipped in and out of the open stores on their skates. I saw plenty of collisions. Even the railing wasn't completely safe. A couple times riders swerved to avoid hitting other bikes and ran right into the rail.

I didn't need to go too far before I got my first job. The owner of one of the small souvenir stores flagged me down and asked me to get him some breakfast. Then Troy at the bingo hall, who looked like he'd partied too much last night, sent me for some medicine for his stomach. I kept pretty busy all morning.

Around eleven one of my errands brought me past the dunk tank. I swung wide when I went by. I didn't know if Malcolm had said anything to Bob yet. I wasn't in the mood to deal with that right now. The bad Bozo, Waldo, was there. The action was so slow that Bob was able to use two hands to eat his peanuts.

I thought about trying to explain things to him. But what was the point? He wouldn't listen to me. He'd listen to Malcolm.

By noon I'd run more than a dozen errands, making a buck or two each time. Twenty-three dollars altogether. I'd hustled the whole morning to make that. Normally, I would've been happy. But I thought about what I'd earned last night. Fifteen dollars for two hours of work. Brutal work. But still—just two hours of it. And thirty dollars the night before.

Maybe you get paid for pain. I guess if I'd tried to run all the errands in two hours, it would have hurt just as much as the two hours I'd spent at the dunk tank.

I didn't know. Right now, I didn't care. I was fried. My head was fuzzy from no sleep. The sun was right overhead. The shadows were short and the air was hot. I was ready to hang out on the beach.

I found Jason at the main volleyball courts near Panic Pier. You could tell the tournament was getting close. There were games at every one of the six courts. Another ten or twelve players stood nearby, waiting for their turn. I went down and sat on top of a small dune off to the side.

He could do it, I thought as I watched Jason play. He was as good as the players we'd seen on TV. The only real difference was that he was younger. But he had two years ahead of him before graduation. He'd just get stronger. And then—look out. I closed my eyes and thought about Jason playing in the big tournaments in Santa Monica. I wanted to believe it would happen. But dreams like that never come true. Mom had had dreams when she came north. They didn't work out. It's always someone else who wins, someone else who lives his dream. Besides, this was Jason's dream. It wasn't mine.

When he'd first mentioned it, freshman year, I'd shared

the fantasy. It was fun to talk about packing up and heading for California. But back then the end of school had seemed impossibly distant. It was safe to pretend. Somehow, we'd talked about it so much that it had turned from a dream into a plan. Jason assumed we were going, and he assumed I was looking forward to it just as much as he was. I couldn't back out on him now without really hurting him. If I was lucky, something would come along that would change his mind.

"Hey," Jason said as he stepped off the court between games. "What's up?"

"Not much. You're looking good. That last spike was awesome."

He shrugged. "Got my rhythm. I'm in the zone. Can't complain. I think we're in good shape for the tournament. We have a real shot at placing in the top three. Maybe even number one."

"That would be great."

"Sure would." He went back for his next game.

I sat and watched them play. My brain was still really fuzzy. Once in a while everything turned flat and far away, like I was watching the world on a movie screen. I might have drifted in and out of sleep for a while, but it didn't help.

Finally, around four o'clock, Jason knocked off. "Ready?" I asked when he came over to me.

"Yeah." He stopped and took a deep breath. "Wow. That was a workout. Come on. Let's see if we can sneak into the pool over at the Sand Buggy."

"Sounds good." The Sand Buggy was a motel near us. We didn't really have to sneak into the pool. The manager was a friend of Jason's dad, and he let us swim there if the pool wasn't crowded.

"I'm not sure I'm working at the tank anymore," I said as we climbed up the steps from the beach and headed down the boardwalk. "As a matter of fact, I'm almost positive I'm not."

"Did you talk to the boss?" Jason asked.

"Not yet. You think there's any point in doing that?"

Instead of answering, Jason said, "Whoa." He staggered like he'd just been kicked. Then he reached up and grabbed his forehead.

"What's wrong?" I asked.

He lowered his hand and took a deep breath. "Nothing."

"You sure?"

"I'm fine." He looked around and frowned, then turned back toward the steps.

"Where you going?" I asked.

"Have to meet Franco. We're practicing."

A weird feeling rippled through my guts, like something extremely wrong was happening. "Jason," I told him, "you just finished practicing. Come on, let's get out of here."

I gave his arm a tug to get him moving. His skin felt cold and his arm dangled loosely in my grip. He didn't even try to pull away. "I think you're still sick or something. Maybe you should just go home. Or come over to my place."

"I feel okay," Jason said. "Couldn't be better. Perfect, as a matter of fact." His voice sounded weird, like he was talking through half a mouthful of wet concrete.

I sped up, wanting to get Jason off the boardwalk before he started acting any stranger. Out of habit, as we passed the Cat-a-Pult, I glanced over, even though I'd accepted the truth that Gwen wasn't coming this year.

But that truth was a lie. "It's her," I gasped as I spotted the unmistakable flash of red hair.

19

Be cool, I told myself as I fought the urge to run over. The last thing she'd want was for some guy to dash up to her, yipping like a puppy dog, panting and drooling. But I had to see if she remembered me. Once I knew that, everything would be great.

"How you doing?" I asked Jason.

"Fine."

"Give me one second, okay?" I steered him toward an empty bench. "I'll be right back."

He slumped onto the bench. "No problem."

"You sure?"

He smiled. "Take your time."

He did sound a bit better. Maybe this was like the other day, just something temporary. I guess all he needed was to rest a minute. If so, the bench was the perfect place for him. I left him there and walked toward the Cat-a-Pult. My lungs felt as if someone had tied a rope around my chest and was pulling it tighter with each step I took. It was nearly impossible to breathe. My heart picked up the rhythm of galloping horses. *Calm down,* I told myself.

It was really her. I moved closer, weaving through the crowd. She was a year older, a year prettier. I watched as she handed a plush lion to a little boy. She bent over and smiled at him, then reached out and ruffled his hair. My thoughts flip-flopped with each step I took. I was sure she'd remember me. I was positive she'd forgotten me.

I moved behind the players and waited for Gwen to notice me. *Stay cool.* She walked to the other side of the stand and set up another kid, taking his money and giving him three stuffed cats. Then she headed back, stooping to gather the scattered cats that had missed the buckets.

I stood in that spot for what seemed like a lifetime. I wanted to say her name, but I was afraid she'd just stare back, puzzled, wondering why some stranger was calling her. Finally, she glanced in my direction. Her eyes caught mine briefly, then slid past.

I searched for the right words. *Hi. Remember me?* But if she said, *No,* what would I do?

A half second later, her head turned back.

"Chad," she said. "It's you. Hi." She smiled and my heart flowed like butter in the sun.

"Hi, Gwen . . ."

She moved quickly to her left, setting up another player, then came back to me. "How are you?"

"Fine. You?"

"Good. Real good."

"You staying for the summer?" I asked, a bit too eagerly.

She started to answer, then her eyes widened. "He's going to get hurt," she said, pointing past my shoulder.

I glanced back. Jason was climbing on top of the bench.

"He's fine," I said. "He just likes to fool around." I figured he was doing it to prove he was feeling better.

"You know him?" she asked.

I nodded. "Best friend." I didn't want to talk about Jason. Not now. "So when did you get here?"

"Yesterday." Gwen pointed at Jason again. "I think your friend has had a little too much of something."

"Honest, there's nothing to worry about."

"If you say so," Gwen said. Then she gasped.

I turned around—and was jolted by the sight of Jason lying flat out on the ground behind the bench. He must have slipped. But he got right back to his feet.

"See," I said, relieved that Jason hadn't really gotten hurt. "He's fine."

Jason climbed back on the bench. People stared at him as they walked by. He started to wobble like he was going to fall again.

Oh, man. "He's just joking around," I said. "He's probably annoyed that I stopped here. We were going swimming. I'll be right back. Don't go away. Okay?"

She laughed. "I'm not going anywhere till my shift is done."

I rushed over to Jason. "Hey, cut it out. You're making me look like a dork."

As he stared down at me, a shiver ran through my body. There was an emptiness behind his eyes. He didn't recognize me. I was sure of that. "Come on," I said. "Get down. I'll take you home."

He looked wildly around, as if he had no idea where he was.

I reached out toward him.

"What's going on here?"

Not now. I turned to face Officers Costas and Manetti. "Nothing's going on," I said.

They stepped closer to the bench. "Get off of there," Officer Costas said.

Jason didn't pay any attention to them.

They grabbed his arms, pulling him down.

"Let me go!" Jason fought to get free, but they pinned him to the bench and slapped handcuffs on his wrists.

This wasn't happening. It had to be a bad dream. I reached out and grabbed Officer Manetti's arm. "Come on. Give him a break. He's sick. It's the flu or something."

"Hey!" My world flipped around with the violence of a coaster ride. I landed flat on my stomach. Rough boardwalk wood pressed against my face. A knee jammed into my back as my arms were yanked behind me. The ratchet sound of the cuffs ended with a sharp pinch against my wrist bones.

Jason was still screaming. One of the cops barked an order into the radio. He was answered by a voice mixed with bursts of static. A string of swear words spilled from my own mouth as I fought against the cuffs. Other cops showed up. They hauled me to my feet, pulled Jason off the bench, and herded us through the staring crowds toward the ramp. I swore and struggled, half blind with rage.

As the cops pushed me along, I caught a glimpse of Gwen watching from the Cat-a-Pult. She had a stuffed cat clenched in her hand.

They led me to the street and shoved me into the backseat of a police car.

"We didn't do anything!" I shouted. But the cops paid no attention.

Officer Manetti showered me with questions. "What are you kids on? How much did you take? You might as well tell us. We're going to find out. Why make it hard on yourselves?"

Jason screamed and kicked out with both feet, rattling the steel mesh that separated us from the cops.

"Calm down, son," Manetti said.

"Animals," Costas snarled. The car lurched as he stomped down on the gas. "I'm not going to listen to this any longer than I have to."

He flipped on the siren. The howl was like a slap in the face, smacking me out of my fury and plunging me into a dreadful reality. Next to me, Jason kept screaming. There was nothing I could do for him. I couldn't even reach out and touch his shoulder. I pulled against the cuffs until my wrists ached and my fingers went numb.

I closed my eyes and wondered whether this could possibly be a nightmare. Mom would die if she had to come get me at the police station, even if I hadn't done anything wrong. Whenever she'd been called to the school, she'd been upset. But this was a million times worse than cutting class or getting into a fight.

Oh, man. A memory floated up from long ago. When I was little, she'd had to go get Dad at the police station. She'd made me wait in the car. They'd pretended nothing had happened. *Your daddy was helping the police with something important,* she'd told me. But I'd heard them arguing about it that night after they thought I was asleep. There's no way I wanted to bring those memories back to her.

We reached the station and the cops dragged us from the car. As we were being marched up the steps, Jason froze. Then his whole body jerked like he'd been shot with a hundred thousand volts. He moved so violently that he broke free from Officer Costas. Before anyone could react, he went limp and collapsed. I saw his eyes roll back as he fell.

"Help him!" I tried to get to Jason, but Officer Manetti held on to my cuffs.

They dragged me inside and locked me in a small room without any windows. Then Costas and Manetti came to talk to me. "Your friend's on the way to the hospital," Costas said. "He could be dying. I've seen it happen often enough. I've seen it all, kid. I've seen punks convulse so bad they bite off their own tongue. Fun, huh? Maybe if the doctors knew what kind of junk your buddy was on, they could save him. Or maybe you just don't care."

"You're wrong," I said.

None of it was right. Jason wasn't dying. And he wasn't on drugs. "He doesn't do that stuff."

I tried to convince them, but it was no use. They wouldn't listen, even though they hadn't found anything when they searched my pockets. They made me write down my phone number. They took my address, too. Then they put me in a cell. And I wasn't alone.

20

THERE WERE TWO GUYS IN THE CELL. A HUGE GUY IN A TANK top and torn denim shorts was passed out face-down on one of the benches that was bolted to the wall. His right arm dangled against the floor. From the mess of his knuckles, I figured he'd been in a fight. The second guy, a skinny old man sitting on the other bench under a small window, glanced up when I came in, then pointed to the huge guy and said, "Shh. Don't disturb Sleeping Beauty."

The door slid shut behind me. When it clanged into place, the sleeper stirred and moaned. I waited until he stopped moving, then walked across the cell and sat near the old guy.

He leaned over and whispered something. I didn't catch it the first time. He said it again. "Saul."

"Chad," I whispered back, offering my hand.

We shook. His grip was bony but a lot stronger than I expected. There didn't seem to be anything else to say. I wondered whether it was okay to ask him why he was here. They did that all the time on TV. But this wasn't some cop show. This was me in big trouble, and I hadn't even done anything. Oh, crap—that's not true. I'd grabbed Officer Manetti's arm. I knew what that was called from TV, too. I'd assaulted an officer.

"Whatcha in for?" Saul asked.

"They haven't told me yet." I left it at that, and he didn't push for any details. After a moment I said, "You?"

"Bank robbery," he answered with a hint of pride in his voice.

I stared at him. He must have been at least seventy, maybe even older. I had a hard time sorting out the decades once people got past forty. "Bank robbery?"

Saul shrugged. "Everybody's got to do something."

"I guess."

"It's what I'm good at. Most of the time, at least." He looked down and shook his head. "I was going to retire next year. Move to Florida. Do a lot of fishing. Maybe rob a little on the weekends."

I wasn't sure if he was kidding me or not.

The next question came out of nowhere. "You got a girl-friend?" Saul asked.

"What?"

He shrugged again. "Just trying to make conversation. Not often you run into someone you can talk with in one of these places."

"Oh."

"So?"

"So what?"

"So, you got a girlfriend?"

Before I could answer, a cop came and slid open the door. "Let's go, Petroff" he said.

"Nice meeting you," Saul said. "Look me up if you ever get down to Fort Lauderdale."

The door clanged shut again, leaving me alone except for the sleeping guy, who didn't look like he'd wake up anytime soon. Then again, I didn't have any idea how long I'd be here. I'd never been arrested. Never been in jail. Didn't even know anyone who'd been arrested, except for Anthony's brother. He'd been busted a whole bunch of times.

Actually, I wasn't even sure if I'd been arrested. Nobody had read me my rights. Nobody had let me make a phone call. I had no idea what was going to happen next, or when it would happen.

I sat and waited. There was nothing else I could do. I kept seeing Jason's face as he passed out on the steps. It couldn't be drugs. Not Jason. He didn't even take cold medicine or aspirin. Vitamins, some protein drinks—that was it.

I kept seeing Gwen's face, too, and the shock in her eyes when the cops dragged me away. I remembered the things I'd screamed at them. I must have seemed like a madman. Gwen would never even want to look at me again.

A wave of anger boiled up inside me. I needed to scream, but I sure as hell wasn't going to risk waking my cellmate. I turned and punched the wall. Stupid move. A dagger of pain sliced through my wrist and up my arm. I closed my eyes and clamped my mouth shut as the sharp burning in my knuckles gave way to a throb. Then I hunched forward, wishing I could just die right there.

No such luck. My heart kept beating. And my mind kept churning, spewing a highlight tape of the worst moments from the past and the future. Jason collapsing, Dad leaving, Dad coming back, Ms. Hargrove sneering at me every day in class, Malcolm glaring at me with all that anger and hatred, the cops looking at me like I was a worthless criminal, the guy from the gift shop pointing at me and shouting that I was a thief. The parade went on and on.

I had no idea how long I stayed that way, trying to shut out the universe, failing to shut out anything.

I didn't bother to look up when the door slid open. I just hugged my knees tighter, figuring the cops had come for the other guy.

"Let's go, kid."

I lifted my head and opened my eyes. The daylight was completely gone. A harsh fluorescent glare from the hallway lit Officer Manetti, who was standing by the open cell door.

"Go where?" I asked.

"You're being released," he said. "It's your lucky day."

I got up from the bench and walked toward the opening, wondering whether he'd slam the bars shut in my face and tell me it was just a joke. Instead, he said something that smacked me harder than any slamming door.

21

"COME ON. YOU DON'T WANT TO KEEP YOUR FATHER WAITING,"
Officer Manetti said. "He looks mad enough already."

"My father?" No. It couldn't be. Not him. Not now. No
way he was ever going to get a chance to be any kind of
hero to me, no matter how much trouble I was in.

"Hey, you're lucky somebody cared enough to come for
you."

Feeling like I'd gotten lost in another person's dream, I
followed Officer Manetti down a long corridor. "What
about my friend?" I asked.

He shook his head. "Sorry. All I know is the ambulance
took him to Mercy General."

"But I can go?"

"There's that little matter of assaulting an officer, but
I'm going to assume it was a misunderstanding. You didn't
intend to grab me—you were trying to grab your friend's
arm. Right? And you missed."

"But I was—"

"You missed," he said again. "Right?"

"Uh, yeah. Right. Thanks."

"Just stay clean," he said. "Really clean. Understand?"

"Yeah . . . yes, sir."

"Look, kid, I got a son your age. I know what it's like.

It's tough being a kid. Especially now. But guess what? It's a lot tougher being a parent. Either way, that's not what matters here. What matters is I gotta do my job. You break the law, I'll bust you. We clear on that?"

I nodded. It was just about the only thing I was clear on right now.

We reached the front desk. I saw him in the waiting area across the room. The words spilled past my lips before my mind figured out what was really going on. "He's not—"

"He's not what?" Officer Manetti asked.

My father. I barely managed to keep the words in. "He's not going to understand," I said, hoping I sounded convincing. "I'll be grounded for the rest of my life."

Officer Manetti sighed. "That's between you and him." He led me past the desk. "Here you go, sir. No charges are being filed. The boy was in the wrong place at the wrong time."

"Thank you, officer," Malcolm said, his anger barely under control. He glared at me, then looked back at Officer Manetti. "I can *assure* you that he will never be any place at the wrong time again."

"I hope not," Officer Manetti said.

Malcolm grabbed my arm and said, "You are in big trouble. Do you have any idea what it feels like to have the police come to the house? Do you have *any* idea? What am I supposed to say to the neighbors?" He dragged me toward the door, ranting the whole time about what sorts of punishment I could look forward to and about how much grief I'd caused him.

We stepped outside into air that had grown hot and humid. But it was better than the air in the cell.

"How was I?" Malcolm asked when we reached the sidewalk. All signs of anger melted away from his face and his voice. "Convincing? Realistic? Did I sell the role of the furious father to the audience? Do you think the part about the neighbors was too much?"

I yanked my arm loose and took a step away from him. "I didn't ask for your help."

"Fine," Malcolm said. "Go back to jail." He walked off.

"Wait." I rushed to catch up with him. "What's going on? What are you doing here?"

"A patrol car came to the house. The cops were looking for the parents of Chad Turner. I just happened to be heading down the front walk when they arrived, so they figured we might be related. They were going to let you sit there until they got in touch with a parent. I had a nice talk with the two officers who brought you here. As far as I can tell, Manetti's not a bad fellow." He let his evaluation of Officer Costas go unspoken. "Anyhow, I promised to take you home."

"Isn't that illegal? Impersonating a parent?"

"You're not the best person to be judging someone right now, are you? Besides, I never made any claims. I just let them believe what they wanted to believe. They were happy to find a volunteer to take you off their hands."

"I can't go home. I have to go see how Jason is." I didn't want to be with Malcolm. I didn't want to owe him anything. Especially after the way I'd set him up with Stinger in the tank.

Malcolm shook his head. "It's past visiting hours. They wouldn't let you see him. When you get home, you can call the hospital and find out how he's doing."

I'd get back a lot faster if I didn't wait for Malcolm. I jogged ahead, then started running. Behind me, I heard him call out, "You're welcome."

I ran until I lost my breath, then jogged, then ran again. I had a long way to go. The police station was far up on First Street. According to the clock I'd seen by the front desk, we'd left there around ten thirty. I figured I'd get home before eleven. After I called the hospital, I could go see if Gwen was still at the Cat-a-Pult. I needed to talk to her right away, before she started dreaming up all kinds of explanations for my behavior.

22

HALFWAY HOME IT STARTED TO DRIZZLE. BEFORE LONG THE drizzle turned into a steady rain. I didn't even bother hunching over. I just let the drops beat down on me and soak in.

By the time I reached the house, it was pouring. Through the curtains I could see Mom at the table, drinking a cup of tea. I stood on the porch for a moment, letting the water drip off me, holding the door open with one hand as I ran the other through my hair.

"You're soaked," Mom said.

"I'm fine. Just got caught in the rain. Jason's sick. He's in the hospital."

Mom set down the cup with a clatter. "What's wrong with him?"

"I don't know. He got sick on the boardwalk, then he just collapsed." I grabbed the phone book from the top of the fridge. The pages blotted up water from my hands and stuck together. Finally, I found the number.

My call was answered on the first ring. "Mercy General. How can I help you?" a woman asked.

"I'm trying to find out about someone."

"What's the patient's name?"

"Jason Lahasca."

"One moment." I heard her put the phone down. A minute later, she said, "He's out of intensive care. They've transferred him to room 387."

"Intensive care!" I said.

Mom came over and put a hand on my shoulder.

"How is he?" I asked.

There was another pause, filled with the clacking of a PC keyboard. "I really don't have any other information at this time," the woman said. "I'm sorry."

"Thanks." I hung up the phone, then dialed Jason's home number.

After four rings the machine answered. "Howdy," Jason's recorded voice said. "We're on the beach. Why aren't you? Leave a message at the beach. I mean, at the beep."

"Nobody's home," I told Mom. I glanced down at our own machine. There was one message on it. I looked back at the table. Mom had her test stuff spread out. She hadn't even thought to check for messages.

"Well, there's nothing you can do tonight," she said. "I'm sure he'll be fine. We'll go to the hospital first thing in the morning, okay?"

"Yeah."

"Why don't you get out of those wet clothes?"

"I will," I said, though I wasn't ready to do that yet. If I couldn't see Jason, I had to at least try to see Gwen. "You aren't going to study all night, are you? You've got to get up early." I opened the fridge and pretended to hunt for a snack, though I wanted to run right out the door.

Mom glanced at the clock. "I didn't realize it was this late." She finished her tea and went to bed. The instant she closed her door, I turned down the volume on the answering machine and played the message. It was from the cops. I erased it, then slipped outside and ran to the boardwalk. I was so wet now that it didn't matter whether I was running in the rain or swimming in the surf. The water flooded over the curb near the end of the block, washing across the sidewalk, lapping at my ankles.

I hoped I could catch Gwen before everything closed down. But as I reached the top of the ramp, a blast of wind slapped me in the face. With that kind of storm sweeping in from the ocean, nothing would be open.

I looked both ways along the boardwalk, squinting against the stinging force of the rain. There wasn't a person in sight. The wind ripped at the signs hanging over the store entrances, swinging them straight out like wings, and swept the water across the boards in overlapping waves. A loud bang startled me as a standing sign blew over.

I put my head down and pushed through the storm, even though I knew it was pointless to go to the Cat-a-Pult. The games and stores were shut tight. The rides, unlit, rose around me like lifeless metal skeletons. The vacationers were tucked safely in their motel rooms, watching the Weather Channel and arguing about who had picked this lousy week to come to the shore.

I reached Wild Willy's Pier. The Bozo tank seemed as dead as everything else on the boardwalk. Nobody was around to stop me. The cops would be out of the rain, just like everyone else. Did the world look any different from the inside? I climbed into the tank and sat on the ledge, dangling my feet in the water. It was nothing to me now. Just another set of bars. Just more water. Just the same wet, miserable world.

"Hey, stupid!" I shouted.

The wind ripped my words away, scattering them like a handful of litter.

"You stupid ass." This time I didn't shout. I didn't have to. The insult was meant for me. I was the mark. I was the clueless loser who'd left his best friend alone on a bench when he needed him the most. Across the way, a sign on a game said ONE WIN CHOICE—boardwalk shorthand for *one win lets you pick whatever prize you want.* Next to it, above a shop entrance, another sign claimed WE HAVE WHATEVER YOU WANT.

No you don't. I grabbed the bars on either side of me. "What do I want?" I said. I didn't know. I wanted Jason to be okay. I wanted Gwen to smile at me again. I wanted Mom to be happy. Those were the things I wanted right now. But what about tomorrow or next year? What did I want? I didn't have a clue. Everyone else knew what they wanted. Everyone. Jason had a goal. Corey had his career all planned out. Mike had the army. What did I have?

A strong gust whipped through the pier, making the poles behind me creak. The rain on the boardwalk crackled like grease in a frying pan.

The faintest sound mingled with the noise of the storm. Laughter. A couple walked by, staying close to the storefronts on the opposite side of the boardwalk, though the overhang gave no shelter against the rain blowing in from the east. The man carried an umbrella that had been ripped inside out and torn to shreds by the wind. They didn't seem to care. They were enjoying the beating that the wind and rain was giving them. Just the two of them.

"It won't last!" I shouted.

The man glanced my way for a moment, but I could tell he didn't see me in the shadows. They walked on past.

Overhead, thunder rumbled. I looked at the iron bars where I clutched them and at the dark water where I dangled my feet, then glared at the sky and shouted, "Go ahead! I dare you!"

But God didn't hurl any lightning bolts to put me out of my misery. He was probably less aware of me than the couple who'd just walked past. I could shout at heaven until my throat bled. It didn't matter. My voice wouldn't even be a whisper in the wind.

After the couple had moved far out of sight, I climbed from the cage. I must have wanted more punishment. I walked on over to the Cat-a-Pult. It was as shut and abandoned as everything else, the prizes packed away, the buckets and sand pit covered with a tarp. The game was dead and dark.

I went back home, dried off, and crawled into bed.

IN THE MORNING MOM DROVE ME THE MILE AND A HALF TO the hospital. The rain had stopped, but the sky was dark with clouds. "Want me to go in with you?" she asked when we reached the parking lot.

"That's okay. You need to get to work. I can walk home." I knew she'd already missed the busiest part of the morning shift. Besides, I was worried that Jason might mention the cops.

"You sure? I'd like to find out how he is."

"I'm sure. I'll call you at the diner as soon as I know anything." I got out of the car and watched her drive off.

A woman at the front desk told me Jason was on the third floor, in the pediatrics ward. I guess that should have been funny, since he's not a little kid. But right now nothing was funny. Not here. A hospital isn't a place people go to for a laugh.

Jason looked awful. At first, when I peeked into the room from the hallway, I wasn't even sure it was him. All I saw was a pale kid hooked up to a bunch of wires and tubes. His skin had that dead look of uncooked chicken.

"Hi." I scrunched up my nose. The room smelled almost too clean. He was alone. There was only one bed. But a purse hanging from the back of a chair told me his mom was nearby.

"Hey . . ." Jason gave a weak nod.

"How you feeling?"

His lips twitched in what might have been a smile. "Been better."

"Chad . . ." someone said from behind me.

I turned to face Jason's parents as they walked in from the hallway.

"What's wrong with him?" I asked.

"The doctors don't know yet," his dad said. He was clutching a Styrofoam cup in one hand. The rim was jagged where he'd torn off small pieces. I noticed the wastebasket was half filled with shredded cups.

His mother, her eyes red, stared at me and said, "Maybe you can tell us."

"I don't know what happened," I said. "Honest. We were heading home. Jason was fine. And then he wasn't."

She looked at me suspiciously, but Jason's dad said, "Nobody's blaming you."

"Thanks." I felt some of the tension drain from me. He'd always been a decent guy. Always treated me well. Even back in freshman year when I'd talked Jason into cutting class. Or last year when we'd gotten caught trying to sneak into a movie. It would be awful if they thought I had anything to do with this.

He wasn't finished. "The important thing is for the doctors to have as much information as possible."

"Right." That made sense. "Jason played a lot of volleyball." I tried to think what else I could tell them.

"Do you remember eating or drinking anything unusual?" Jason's dad asked.

"No." I thought back. "Nothing."

Jason's dad lowered his voice. "Maybe one of your friends gave you boys some pills?"

"Pills? No way." I shook my head. This was getting very uncomfortable. I glanced at Jason for support, but he looked like he was drifting off.

"Just tell me, okay?" his dad said. "You won't get in trouble. But we have to know."

"We didn't take anything. I swear!" I realized I was shouting. This was crazy. I'd told the truth. It wasn't my fault that they didn't believe me.

"There's more going on here than a couple beers," Jason's dad said.

Not that again. One morning last summer, on the way to Jason's place, I'd passed a rental house where there'd been a major party. I found half a six-pack on the lawn. I'm not even sure why I picked it up. I don't like beer. The smell reminds me of my dad. But I brought the cans with me. Jason didn't want them, either. We didn't even bother to hide them. I just put them on his desk and we got involved with other stuff. When his mom saw them, she flipped out on us. I told her right away that they were mine, so Jason wouldn't get in trouble. She'd been pretty angry with me, and she'd stayed angry for almost a month.

Jason's dad looked like he planned to keep asking questions. There was no way I was going to hang around while he grilled me.

"I gotta go," I said. I rushed into the hall and headed toward the elevator.

I hadn't gone more than a couple steps when it hit me. Oh, crap. Now I really looked guilty because I was running off. I couldn't win. If I stayed, they'd treat me like a criminal. If I left, they'd think I'd done something wrong. I turned toward the door, wondering if I should go back.

As I stood there trying to decide what to do, a doctor brushed past me and went into the room. I stayed where I was and listened.

"There is some good news," he said. "We've ruled out a stroke."

"A stroke?" Jason's mom said. "He's only sixteen."

"Some of the symptoms were there," the doctor said. "The confusion, the partial paralysis. The same symptoms can occur with what we call a transient ischemic episode, where a clot passes through the brain. Those can happen for many reasons. But there's also evidence of an Addisonian crisis. Right now, the numbers for his adrenal hormones—"

"You can make him better, can't you?" Jason's mom asked.

There was a pause. "Whatever is going on, it involves more than just his adrenal glands," the doctor said. "Other systems seem to be under stress. His lungs are involved. Possibly his kidneys. We'll just have to keep running tests."

"He's an athlete," Jason's mom said. "He's in great shape. He exercises every day. He can't be sick. You should talk to that boy he was with. Chad Turner. Ask him. Then you'll find some answers."

I hurried away, the doctor's words echoing in my mind. Brain, lungs, kidneys . . .

I called Mom from a phone in the lobby, then left the hospital. Normally, I'd take the long way home, swinging over to Atlantic Avenue so I wouldn't have to go near Abbot Drive. Right now I didn't care. I went through the heart of the bad area, past overgrown yards guarded by growling dogs, ignoring the people who called out with offers to sell me whatever I wanted. What I wanted, you couldn't buy here. Or anywhere.

When I got home, I realized none of our friends knew about Jason. I called Corey and told him what had happened.

"You're kidding," he said after a long silence.

"I wish I was."

"He looked fine last time I saw him," Corey said.

"I know. That's the scary part."

"Yeah, it makes you think anyone could just drop dead right in front of you. When my grandma visits, I'm always afraid she'll die as soon as my folks leave the house. She takes these naps, and I keep checking to see if she's breathing."

"You're warped," I said. "You know that?"

"I'm sadly aware of my failings," Corey said. "Is there anything we can do for him?"

"I don't know. I wish there was. Look, I'll call you if there's news," I told him. "I'm going to see Ellie." I hung up the phone and headed out the door.

I found Ellie in the lifeguard chair near the boathouse. In front of us the waves, still stirred up from last night's storm, crashed against the beach, churning the sand into a muddy, frothy mix. There was hardly anyone around. Even so, Ellie never stopped scanning the water while we talked, checking on the few people who'd waded past their ankles in the surf.

"That's awful," she said when I'd given her the details. "How can we help?"

I shrugged. The question had been on my mind ever since Corey'd asked it. "I don't know. Visit, I guess. I could buy him some magazines." None of that sounded like it would make much difference. I really didn't have a clue. I'd never had a friend in the hospital before.

"We have to do *something*," Ellie said. She glanced at her watch. "I'll go visit him as soon as my shift is over."

"Great. He'll appreciate that. I'm going to find Mike." I headed up to the boardwalk.

I passed the Cat-a-Pult. It was too early for Gwen to be working. I looked at the bench by the railing and flinched as I remembered how I'd been slammed to the ground and dragged off, screaming and struggling like a lunatic. I wondered whether anyone in the crowd recognized me. There were people out there who were going to know I looked familiar. They'd stare and dig for the memory that matched the face. *Wasn't that the kid the cops dragged off? Stay away from him. He's probably stoned.* At least most of them were only here for a week. They'd be gone soon enough. I wished they could take the memory away with them. Take it from me so I wouldn't have to live with it.

I found Mike running the BB game—the one where you try to shoot out a red star from the middle of a paper target. It was an honest game—just really hard. Mike wasn't busy. And even with a crowd, it was an easy game to run since all you had to do was take the money and load the guns. The BBs were already in a tube. You just popped the cap and poured the ammo into the rifle. After that, the only hard part was arguing with the players who mistakenly thought they'd won. You had to shoot out every single bit of the red star. If even one tiny piece was left, you lost. People have a hard time seeing those little bits of red when they're the difference between a win and a loss.

"That sucks," Mike said when I'd told him. "You think he'll be there long?"

"I hope not. But he didn't look like he was going anywhere for a while. The doctors haven't even figured out what's wrong yet."

"Let me know if I can do anything," Mike said.

"Sure."

"Hey, I won!" a guy shouted, pointing to the target in front of him. Even from where I stood I could see he'd missed a ton of red. I waved bye to Mike and left him to do his job.

I hunted for some errands to keep me busy. I worked for a couple hours, then headed back home. By the time I got there, it was starting to rain again. It wasn't as heavy as yesterday, but it had the feel of rain that was going to last for a while. At least through the rest of today. Maybe tomorrow, too.

I called the hospital and asked for Jason's room. His mom answered.

"He's asleep," she told me.

As I was trying to think of something to say, she hung up.

I blew the rest of the afternoon watching television. Then I walked out to the Cat-a-Pult to see if Gwen was around. But there was just one girl at the booth. A lot of the games cut down their crews during bad weather.

The rain kept up through the evening and into the morning. There was still a light rain falling the next afternoon when I walked to the hospital, but the forecast called for the weather to clear sometime after midnight.

Jason's folks were sitting in two chairs pulled up next to the bed. I didn't want to be around them, but I needed to see Jason.

He looked the same. No better, no worse. He nodded when I came in, and managed to say, "Hi."

"Hi." I looked over at his mom and dad. "Okay if I stay for a little?"

His mom ignored me. His dad said, "Yeah, sure."

"Did the doctors figure anything out?"

They didn't answer me.

"No drugs, right?"

No answer. But that was enough to tell me Jason's blood tests had come back clean. If anything had showed up, his parents would have been all over me. Even so, they still acted like everything was my fault. I guess they had to blame somebody. I just wished it wasn't me.

I talked with Jason for a while. Mostly I talked and he listened. There wasn't a lot to talk about. The tournament was less than two weeks away, but I didn't want to mention it. What if he wasn't out of the hospital by then? That would be awful. He'd been waiting all year for it. I knew what that felt like.

So I just talked without really saying much of anything. I noticed Jason's dad kept looking out the window. After a while he said. "There's no way I can do it."

I kept talking to Jason, but I also listened while his dad talked to his mom.

"I've got three roofs I'm supposed to finish this week," he said. "The rain's put me way behind. We won't even be able to get started until tomorrow."

"It'll be all right," Jason's mom said. "You've always managed."

"I'd be fine if I could hire a couple extra guys. But there's no way I can find skilled men by tomorrow. With the storm and all, everyone's already got jobs lined up." He walked back over to the window and leaned against the sill.

I knew Jason's dad didn't want anything to do with me, and he'd probably shoot me down the moment I opened my mouth, but I had to give it a try. I turned away from Jason and said, "I can help."

Jason's dad looked at me but didn't say anything.

"I'm free tomorrow. I can help out with the roofing jobs."

"Haven't you helped enough?" Jason's mom asked.

I could see there was no point in talking with them. I turned back to Jason. Maybe I could get him to convince them I hadn't done anything.

"Ever nailed shingles?" his dad asked. He moved away from the window and walked toward me.

"Sure. You and Jason showed me how last August. Remember when you were doing the house next door to yours? So you want me to help?"

"I don't think so." He shook his head. "It's nice of you to offer, but it's still not going to be enough to get the jobs done on time."

"I could call a couple friends," I said. "I'm sure Mike can get a day off, and I know Corey's around."

At the mention of Corey, Jason let out a sound that might have been a laugh. I had to admit, the thought of Corey on a ladder was funny. The thought of Corey anywhere near tools was pretty funny, too. I looked at Jason and said, "Knowing him, he'll bring a parachute."

Jason laughed weakly, then gave a single, quiet cough.

Beneath the sickness, I could see a faint sign that the real Jason existed. Weak but still there. He closed his eyes again.

"What do you have to lose?" I asked Jason's dad.

"Everything, if one of you kids gets hurt," he said.

"We'll be fine. Give us a chance. Between the three of us, we can probably do enough to free up one of your guys for the skilled work. Maybe even two. Right?"

He sighed, then nodded. "Okay, Chad. We'll try it. Thanks. I'll pick you up at five. The job I can put you on is way out toward Philly."

Five? Oh, lord. I'd forgotten what time roofers started work. "Great. Perfect. I'll be ready. You won't be sorry."

I asked if I could use the phone, then called Mike. He was more than happy to help out. Corey was less happy, but I talked him into it after reminding him how Jason had saved him from getting beaten up at a dance last year. And at two different football games. And a couple times after school. And once in the cafeteria. I promised Corey he wouldn't have more than one foot off the ground at any time.

Since it was just for a day, and since it was a favor for a friend's dad, I figured Mom wouldn't have any problem with me doing the roofing work. She made some worried sounds when I mentioned it that evening, but she gave in pretty easily.

Jason's dad picked me up at five the next morning. He had an old junker van he used to take his crews to jobs. No seats except for the driver. I climbed in the back and sat on the floor. There were already four guys there. They nodded in my direction, then ignored me. We swung by Mike's place. Corey was there with him. So was Ellie, who had a tool belt buckled on over her work pants.

"I took the day off, Mr. Lahasca," she told Jason's dad.

"Great. Glad to have you," he said. He opened the back door of the van. "You're really saving my hide."

"Mike called me," Ellie explained as she came around. She stared at the roofers, who were staring at her. "Something wrong?" she asked.

A couple of the men snickered. "We ain't baking cakes," one of them said.

Ellie sighed and reached into the van. She grabbed a scrap piece of two-by-four and tossed it to the curb. "Neither am I," she said as she pulled a hammer from its loop and plucked a handful of nails from a pocket of the belt. She dropped to one knee. Then, with a single awesome whack, she drove a nail all the way into the wood. All the way. I knew I couldn't come close to doing that.

She knocked in two more nails just as easily, then looked around and said, "May I join you? Pretty please?"

"Only if you promise to put that hammer away." I slid over and made room for her. "Where'd you learn to do that?"

She grinned. "You pick up all kinds of things when you're raised in a house full of brothers."

Mike, Corey, and Ellie got in, and the van drove off.

We got started before six thirty. I think roofers enjoy waking people up. They didn't even ring the bell to warn anyone. They just slapped a couple ladders against the gutter, climbed up, and started clomping around in their work boots, ripping off the old shingles. From the way they smiled at each other, I could tell they enjoyed being human alarm clocks.

Before long I discovered how brutal roofing can be. It made working at the Bozo tank seem like a vacation. The sun came out with a vengeance. Thanks to the light soaking into the black tarpaper, the temperature felt like it was 700 degrees. Of course, there wasn't any shade on the roof. I'd have traded my left arm for a chance to plunge into a tank of water.

By quitting time, I felt I'd been run through a meat grinder. Or maybe a deep fryer. We didn't even knock off until it got too dark to see. But we finished the job.

"Well," I said to Mike as we rode back, "I know another thing I don't want to do for a living."

Mike opened his mouth to answer me, but all that came out was a moan.

"I'd rather wrestle sharks," Ellie said.

"It wasn't that bad," Corey said. That was true, at least for him. He'd been on the ground the whole day. The only time he'd raised a sweat was when he had to dodge whatever we tossed down at him.

"Not bad at all," he added.

I bent over and grabbed Ellie's hammer. "I got enough strength for one more swing," I said.

"Okay, okay—it was bad for you guys," Corey said.

I put down the hammer and leaned back.

"Thanks, Chad," Jason's dad said when he pulled up at the house to drop me off. "You and your friends made a big difference." He dug for his wallet, but I wouldn't take any money.

"Glad I could help."

He nodded. "I'm glad you could, too." Close up, I could see he was exhausted.

"Look. Jason's going to be okay," I said. "I know it."

He gave me a tired smile and drove off. I went inside and

collapsed on the couch. I figured I'd rest up a bit, then see if I could find Gwen. Now that the weather was nice, she had to be back at the Cat-a-Pult.

The next thing I knew, it was morning. I opened my eyes to a room filled with daylight. Mom was gone. I checked the clock. It was after ten.

I couldn't believe I'd blown my chance to go to the boardwalk. I got up, then fell back to the couch as my body reminded me I'd spent a whole day working on a roof. I tried again, more slowly, and managed to make my way the short distance to the fridge. I was starving.

After I ate, I walked to the hospital. By now I figured the doctors would know what was wrong with Jason. But when I got there it was pretty obvious nothing had changed. He still looked awful.

His dad was out at work. But his mom was there. I waited by the door, expecting her to tell me to get lost. She glanced up, then looked away without saying anything, which I figured was about as close to an invitation as I was going to get. Maybe my time on the roof had been enough to move her from hating me to merely disliking me.

"I have to run some errands. I'll be back soon," she said to Jason a moment later. "I'll leave you and your *friend* alone." She went out. I figured she probably needed a break. Or maybe she just didn't want to be around me.

Jason had a small TV mounted on the wall in the corner. Someone had also wheeled an entertainment cart into the room—it held a monitor hooked up to a VCR and an old Super Nintendo. A sticker on the side said it was a gift to the hospital from one of the big stores in the mall. Games and tapes were stacked on a shelf under the set.

"Want to watch a movie?" I asked.

Jason gave a weak shrug.

I checked out the videos. *Memories of Love*. Didn't sound promising. Probably no good car chases or fistfights. I read the back. Crap. All about a guy whose girlfriend dies. I checked the next one. *A Time Before We Parted*. Woman's daughter dies. No way. *My Girl*. I'd seen that. Girl's boyfriend dies. A quick scan through the rest of the pile showed it was a choice between orphans, the dead, and the doomed. Forget it. I wasn't going to sit in a hospital watching movies where people died.

"We could play a game," I said.

Jason shook his head. "You go ahead." He pushed the button, raising the back of the bed halfway up to a sitting position.

I popped in Super Mario World. While I played, I told Jason about my day on the roof, and about everyone throwing stuff at Corey. That got a small chuckle out of him. I did an imitation of Corey trying to be useful without climbing a ladder.

Jason laughed and shook his head. "Wish I'd seen that."

"I'll bring a camera next time. Though I hope there isn't a next time."

I sat there, talking away, keeping Jason company and watching Mario plunge to his death whenever I missed a jump. After a while Jason fell asleep. I stayed in my seat by his bed, not wanting him to wake up alone. A little after noon, a doctor came in to check on him. He picked up a chart from the end of the bed and wrote something on it. He was pretty young for a doctor. I wondered how good he was. I wondered if he was good enough to help Jason.

"WHAT'S WRONG WITH HIM?" I ASKED.

The doctor replaced the chart, then glanced over at me. "Friend of yours?"

"No, I'm a weirdo who gets a kick out of sitting in hospital rooms with strangers."

I expected the doctor to just blow me off without an answer, but he came over and sat in the chair next to me. "I guess that was a stupid question."

I shrugged. "You going to tell me what's wrong with him?"

"If I knew that, I'd be a very happy man."

"So you don't know?"

He shook his head. "I know what's wrong, but not why. We can treat the *what,* but that's not going to help your friend a whole lot unless we can fix the *why.*"

It took me a second to figure out what he was saying. I nodded to show him I was following the explanation.

"I'm not supposed to give medical information to anyone except family members," the doctor said. "But in this case, it's more a matter of things we don't know, so I guess I can talk with you about it."

"Thanks."

"The problem is in his immune system," the doctor said.

"Oh, man . . ." I knew what that meant.

"Don't jump to conclusions," he said. "I'm not talking about AIDS. Your friend's problem isn't a weakened immune system; it's an overactive system. You know how the body fights infection?"

"Yeah." We'd had that in biology class. "White cells and all that sort of stuff."

"Right. But Jason's body is fighting against *itself*, attacking healthy cells. He has an autoimmune disease. There are all kinds. Some are serious, some are mildly annoying."

"We're not talking annoying here, are we?"

The doctor shook his head. "Multiple organs are involved—lungs, kidneys, maybe others. And something in the circulatory system that ended up throwing a clot."

"Oh, crap."

"Yeah, 'Oh, crap' is right. There are more accurate medical terms, but that sums it up pretty well." He glanced at Jason. I guess to make sure he was still asleep.

"So now what?"

"We need to stabilize his condition, and we need to figure out why his body is attacking itself." He sighed and stood up.

I was glad he hadn't treated me like some dumb kid. "Thanks for explaining that stuff to me."

He nodded and started to walk out, then glanced back and said, "You can help. Attitude is important. Do what you can to keep his spirits up."

"I will." But I didn't know if anything I did would make a difference.

I waited until Jason's mom got back. It was obvious from the way she stared through me that she still blamed me for everything. There wasn't much I could do about that. I said good-bye and left.

On the walk home I tried to think of ways to cheer Jason up. He always liked to talk about California. Maybe I could bring in some road maps or a tour book or something. And if—I mean, when—he got better, we'd do it. After we finished school, we'd buy a car and head out for the beach at Santa Monica. Jason would play in tournaments, and I'd find something to do. There had to be tons of jobs out there. Mom would have her certificate by then, so she'd be okay. Maybe she could even come out with us.

I felt that as long as I kept the plan alive I'd be keeping Jason alive. Even if I didn't share the dream.

What about my dreams? What about Gwen? I sped up as I realized she might be working right now. I cut across to Thirty-fifth Street and climbed up the ramp to the boardwalk.

She was there at the booth. I stood near the ramp for a while, watching her and wondering what she thought of me. The last time she'd seen me, I'd been a screaming madman surrounded by cops.

Taking a deep breath, I walked over to the Cat-a-Pult.

26

I WATCHED HER FACE CAREFULLY WHEN HER EYES MET MINE, hoping to see a smile. All I got was a cautious nod.

"Can I explain?" I asked.

"Go ahead." There was no emotion in her voice.

I told her about Jason getting sick. And I told her that I'd come right back to see her but the storm had closed the game down.

She listened to everything, her expression barely changing. When I finished, I felt like I was waiting for a jury to read a verdict. In my heart I hoped she'd tell me she understood. *Not guilty.* In my gut I was afraid she'd tell me to go away. *Guilty on all charges.*

"That must have been awful," she said.

"It was."

"I hope your friend is okay."

"Me, too." I sensed there was something else coming.

"It's bad to lose your temper," she said.

"I know." I couldn't argue with that.

"My sister married a guy who lost his temper a lot." Gwen sighed and stared past me toward the ocean. "She left him, but not before he broke her jaw and three of her ribs."

A cold anger washed over her face as she spoke. I desperately needed to tell her that I couldn't even imagine doing something like that. Whatever else my dad had done, he hadn't ever hit my mom. That was one inheritance I didn't have to fear.

"The stuff with the cops—that's never happened before," I said. "It was just—" I paused, not sure of the right way to tell her why I'd acted so crazy. How could I say I'd dreamed of her all winter? How could I explain that the cops had dragged me off just when I'd finally found her again? How could I explain without sounding like a pathetic lovesick puppy?

"You were worried about your friend," she said, finishing my sentence.

I nodded. That was true, too. "Yeah. It was pretty awful. By the time they got us to the station, I thought he was dying."

She shuddered, and her expression softened a bit. "You really care about him. He's lucky to have you for a friend."

"I'm the lucky one," I said. "Jason's a great guy." I felt that I was on a tightrope. If I tried too hard to prove how much I cared, I'd sound like a phony. *Just be yourself,* I thought. Right now I wasn't even sure what that meant. Maybe Malcolm wasn't the only actor. Maybe everyone acted all the time. We acted one way with friends, another with parents, another with cops, another with teachers. And another with beautiful girls . . .

I kept talking, telling her about the hospital and the doctor, and even about my day on a roof. Somehow we slipped slowly past the awkwardness. After a while Gwen smiled. Then she laughed. She worked while we talked. And I tried to work up the courage to ask her out. This time I wasn't going to let the chance slip away. But I didn't think today was the right day. It was too soon. I felt we were still mending the cracks. There was time. Nearly the whole summer lay ahead.

"Maybe I'll see you tomorrow," Gwen said when her shift ended.

"I'll be around," I told her.

"I hope your friend's okay."

"Thanks."

I watched her leave the booth. My body felt like it had been set free from a clamp that had been slowly tightening since yesterday. Maybe everything really would be all right. If Gwen could come back—come all the way here from Montana—and I could find her, then maybe Jason could get better. Maybe Mom could finish her classes and find a job she liked. Maybe hope wasn't such a bad thing to have.

Once Gwen moved out of sight, I wandered along the boardwalk, weaving through the crowds, and made my plans for tomorrow. After I visited Jason, I'd come back to the Cat-a-Pult and ask Gwen out. Somewhere special. Maybe really splurge and take her for lobster.

I realized this could be an expensive summer. I needed to build up my spare cash, so for the rest of the afternoon and evening I hustled small jobs, losing myself in the work. But I didn't go near the Bozo tank. I wanted to give Bob more time to cool off from whatever Malcolm had told him. I'd wait a couple days and then go talk to him. I might even get brave and tell him I wanted to work in the tank. I was feeling lucky.

The next morning Jason was alone. His mom had had to go back to her office. That was a bad sign. It meant Jason wasn't there for a short stay—like when you have your tonsils out. Life was going on around him, getting back to normal, but leaving him here in this hospital bed. Like water flowing past a rock in a river. Nobody really knew when he'd get out.

There were half a dozen cards taped to the wall opposite the bed, along with a shiny helium-filled balloon. "Someone visit?" I asked.

"Couple girls from school," Jason said. He stopped to take a breath. "Julia, her friends. The usual crowd."

"That must have been nice." I figured seeing them should have cheered him up.

He shrugged. "I guess."

Or maybe it just made him feel worse, watching them come and go while he was stuck in here.

"I'm going to ask Gwen out," I said, changing the subject.

"About time."

I didn't tell him the details of my plans. I figured he wouldn't want to hear that I'd be eating lobster while he was choking down toast and tapioca pudding. But I'd brought something I knew he'd want to see.

"Look what I have," I said, holding up the road map. I spread it open on the bed and talked about some of the places we'd pass through on our trip across the country. I'd also brought one of those free magazines with all the used-car ads. We'd already agreed that the best possible set of wheels for any trip was a Mustang convertible. Year and price range were open to debate.

As I charted our path, I kept thinking about what the doctor had told me. *Keep his spirits up.* The worst part—

and it made me feel truly rotten—was that I didn't want to be there, sitting in this room that smelled too clean, watching the doctors and nurses shuffle in and out, wondering what I could possibly say that would make any difference.

I wanted to be with Gwen. I guess that made me a really awful friend. But I stayed all morning. So maybe that made me an okay friend. Or maybe not. A good friend would want to be there. I guess mostly it just made me crazy.

At one point, while I was reading car ads to him, I realized he hadn't said anything for a while. I glanced over, half expecting him to be asleep. But his eyes were open. He was staring up at the ceiling. "You okay?" I asked.

"I'm never going to get better," he said after a long silence.

"Sure you are. Don't talk that way." I couldn't imagine him staying there, pale and weak, stuck full of tubes and needles.

He shook his head. "Gonna miss the tournament."

That was looking pretty true, but I didn't want him to lose hope. The one thing I could do for him—the only thing—was to try to keep him from giving up. "You still have time. They pump you full of the right drugs, you'll be as good as new."

"At least you're off the hook," he said.

"What are you talking about?"

"California." He pushed the map away. "You never really wanted to go there with me."

I felt like I'd been caught stealing. *How could he know?* This was no time for the truth. "Sure I want to go. I'm looking forward to it." Damn, I could hear the stress in my voice. I was a lousy liar.

Jason shook his head. "You were just—" He stopped as a wave of coughing hit him. ". . . pretending . . . 'cause I wanted . . ."

"No, it would be great. It *will* be great. You and me. Santa Monica. We're gonna do it." I told him every lie I could dream up about the bright future that we'd make for ourselves. It didn't work. He closed his eyes and turned his head away. After a while he drifted off to sleep, leaving me alone with my guilt.

As I listened to him breathing in shallow gasps, I thought about a book we'd read last year in school. *Of Mice and Men*. One guy, George, was always telling the other, Lenny, about their plans. They were going to buy a farm and raise rabbits. That was their dream. That was all they had. It was a really good book, but it was also a really sad one. I hoped Jason would have more than a dream.

Jason's mom came by at lunchtime. She gave me the same look she might have used if she'd discovered that the neighbor's dog had dropped a load in the middle of her porch. As I left the room, I heard her follow me into the hallway.

"You don't have to visit him every day," she said.

"I like seeing him," I said. "He's my friend."

She shook her head. "Let me make this clear. You're bad for him. I never could understand what he saw in you. Right now it's not his choice to make. It's mine. He needs rest. He doesn't need some little thug hanging around getting him all worked up."

A million answers flashed through my mind. But beneath them all, the fear that she was right sealed my lips. I turned away and left the hospital, promising myself I'd visit

Jason again in a couple days, after his mom had more of a chance to cool off. I thought about just going home, but I couldn't let my other plans die. The day had started out badly enough. I needed to do something I could feel good about.

I headed for the boardwalk. The Cat-a-Pult was crowded, so I said hi to Gwen but didn't hang around. If I bugged her too much when things were busy, she might start thinking I was a nuisance. Last year Corey'd had this crush on Beverly Buckley. He kept talking to her every chance he got. One day during lunch she blew up and shouted at him to stay out of her face. It wasn't a pretty scene. Corey was devastated. If Gwen did that to me, I think I'd die.

I ran errands for a couple places near the Cat-a-Pult, just to help kill the time, and then returned to my spot behind the players. Whenever things were slow there, I talked with Gwen, but I backed off as soon as it got busy.

She took a fifteen-minute break at two o'clock. We walked and talked. She wanted to study art when she went to college. "Maybe in Chicago," she said. "But I'm not sure if I could live in a big city. Our town's real small. I know just about everyone."

"I don't even know half the people on my block," I said. "People are always moving in and out around here."

"If someone moves into our neighborhood," she said, "my mom bakes them a cake."

"Sounds nice."

She nodded. "Sometimes it's the little things that you re-member. Even years later."

That was sure true. I wondered if she remembered the

first time we'd met. But I didn't want to bring up the past right now, especially since I'd spent so much of it doing stupid things. Instead, I turned our conversation in other directions, trying to learn all I could about her.

She liked pistachio ice cream. She thought football was okay but would rather watch soccer. She didn't have a favorite video game. We both liked the same rock bands. She wasn't a big fan of sea gulls. She'd read *Of Mice and Men,* too, and suggested a couple books I might enjoy. She also mentioned a short story called "Araby." She said it was her favorite and I could borrow her copy of the book it was in. She thought I was lucky to live near the ocean all year round. I filed each scrap of information.

Part of me wanted desperately to spend every moment with her. Another part kept whispering that I didn't deserve even an instant of pleasure while Jason was lying in the hospital, wasting away. I looked for a chance to ask her out but kept finding reasons to wait. Then, all too soon, she went back to work. And I went back to hovering.

Around four, she glanced at her watch and said, "One more hour."

"You get off at five?" I asked.

"Yeah. Then I come back at seven." She nodded over toward the boy working the booth with her. "It's slow enough between five and seven for one person to handle it."

No more excuses, I told myself. I'd ask her out when she left the booth. Make the whole thing casual. Just stroll along with her. Mention food. Mention that I was hungry. Wait for her to say something, then take it from there. *Hey, I know a good place around the corner. Want to grab a bite? My treat.* I could do it. She'd be really surprised when she found out that "the place around the corner" had awesome lobster dinners.

I stepped away as a group of players came by. Then I went for a walk because I was too nervous to stand around and wait. When I came back, I stopped at a railing a half block south of the Cat-a-Pult. To my right, the Sea Devil coaster roared past on a corkscrew curve banked so steeply all I saw was the bottom of the cars. The screams of the riders barely rose above the clatter of the wheels.

I thought about the first drop on that ride. The worst part was the long wait while the cars crawled 120 feet up the slope. Then, after you crested the top, everything plunged toward the earth—everything except your stomach, which rushed to catch up. Before you knew it, you were at the bottom and shooting into the first corkscrew. The rest was easy.

One time, I thought. I just had to get through asking Gwen out one time. Climb that first steep hill and take one stomach-wrenching plunge. After that it would be easy.

A couple minutes before five, I headed toward the Cat-a-Pult, ready to step free from the safety of silence.

Gwen was chatting with someone. His back was to me, but as I got closer, I recognized him with a jolt that felt like a knife slicing straight through my body. Slicing and twisting. Oh, man, not him. What was *he* doing here? I hesitated, wondering whether to wait for him to leave. But Gwen's shift would end any minute now. I had to talk to her before she went off.

As I reached them, Anthony glanced at me and grinned. "Hey, Ballzo! What's up?"

I managed to nod, then looked at Gwen, wondering what in the world was going on.

"Chad, do you know Anthony?" she asked. There was something odd in her voice.

"Yeah . . ."

"Chad and I go way back," Anthony said. He slapped me on the back. "So you know each other? Small world. I just met Gwen a couple days ago. Right before the big storm."

When I was sitting in jail, I thought.

"Hey, man," Anthony said, "I heard your friend's in bad shape. Tough break. Sometimes life really sucks." He seemed amused. I wanted to smash his face.

Gwen glanced at her watch. "Five o'clock." She sat on the ledge between two of the catapults and swung her legs over the counter. "Anthony asked me to go get something to eat," she said. She looked at me, and then at Anthony. "He asked me yesterday, before you stopped by."

Anthony grinned. "Hey—I'd invite you to join us, but I got a table for two at *La Tratoria.* You know how it is. These classy places don't like changing reservations. Besides, it wouldn't be any fun for you, since you don't have a date. Maybe some other time."

"Well, see you later, Chad," Gwen said as she left with him.

Anthony walked a couple steps away, then looked back at me and winked. "Stay out of trouble, Ballzo."

I watched them go off together. Anthony and Gwen. Anthony, with his bottomless supply of drug money and his ability to ruin every decent thing he ever touched. Gwen, with her smile and her grace, and my heart.

It couldn't be happening.

I wanted to sink down through the boardwalk, and then

through the sand, and keep sinking down through what-ever else lay between me and the center of the earth. Not him. It was unbearable that she was going away with some-one else. It was beyond unbearable that she had chosen Anthony. Couldn't she see he was nothing but trouble?

"I won, Mommy! Look! I won!"

A little girl with bright blond pigtails and a sunburned face shouted and jumped as she pointed to where her cat had landed head down in the bucket.

"That's wonderful, dear," her mom said.

"I'm so proud of you," her dad said. He bent and gave her a hug as a cat yowl blared through the speakers. "You're my special little girl. I'm so glad the three of us came here."

I wanted to go see Jason. But his mom would be there. My mom was off at school. Alone, I turned and shuffled toward my house, walking into a gray place and time that sealed over me like the lid of a coffin.

27

SOMEONE HAD DRILLED A LARGE HOLE THROUGH EVERY VITAL part of me. All spirit, all life, had drained out, leaving a shell that might have blown away in the wind if I'd stepped from the house. There was no danger of that. My universe shrank to the size of the couch. I sat there, or slept there. With or without the drone of the television. Sometimes I just stared at the wall. Mom came and went. I guess, at first, she assumed I was tired. We must have talked. I remember conversations. But they were like old movies, black-and-white—the sound faded to the point where the words themselves were nothing more than another part of the fog.

Mom's voice grew worried at some point. I told her I was okay. Just sad about Jason. She'd spoken with his folks. The doctors had a name for the disease. But that didn't help. They were trying everything they could think of. Mike or Corey called once in a while. I stopped answering the phone. They dropped by. More gray images I couldn't sort out.

June gave way to July. It was all the same to me. Nothing changed but the page on the calendar that hung near the clock. It had been a photo of a sunrise. Now it was a lighthouse. The tournament came and went. That must have been a rough day for Jason—rougher than the others—but

I didn't have room for other people's losses in the dead world I'd entered. More days. More visits. Mike, Corey, and Ellie. The voices blended. The message remained the same.

Chad, man, you've got to get up.

No, I don't.

You can't spend the rest of your life on the couch.

Why not?

Get off that couch or I'll kick your butt.

Go ahead. . . .

They talked, shouted, pleaded, joked. It was all nothing but a murmur. Corey tried to give me a sheet of paper. I wasn't interested. He ended up tossing it across the room. It fluttered to the floor. Finally, they left. Friends. I had friends who cared. That wasn't enough to lift the weight that crushed me down. Not even close.

A couple days later, freakin' Malcolm showed up. Maybe Mom had asked him to talk to me. Maybe not. It didn't matter. I ignored the knock. He came in anyhow.

"I've got a wake-up call for Chad Turner," he said in a sickeningly cheerful voice.

The light spilling through the open door made me flinch. I turned face-down on the couch, wishing he'd just go away.

Another voice. This time a little boy. "Can Chad come out and pway? Pwease?"

I ignored him while he chattered away, switching from one cartoon character to another. Then he started talking in his normal voice. "Hey, Chad, I just spoke to Bob. He's going to have an opening in early August. One of the guys is quitting."

I didn't care. I didn't want to listen. But Malcolm kept jabbering. "I think I can get you his spot. It'll take some work. There's a lot to learn. You only have three weeks to get ready. What do you say?"

I just lay where I was, sucking dusty air through the couch cushions. *Keep your charity,* I thought, but it wasn't worth the effort to speak the words.

"What do you say, Chad?"

I didn't say anything.

"Chad, this is a great opportunity."

I lifted my face half an inch from the cushions and told him to leave. I added a couple words I'd never say around my mom.

I put my head back down and waited for the sound of footsteps and a closing door. Instead, I heard a loud grunt. An instant later, the world jolted on its side and I rolled across the floor. Malcolm had tipped the couch over.

He stood there, panting from the sudden effort. Maybe panting from the rush of anger he'd have needed to move the couch. It weighed a ton. He'd actually flipped it over.

"You're crazy!" I shouted.

"You make me sick!" he shouted back.

I stood up and pointed at the door. "Get out."

He didn't move. "You really make me sick. Just give up and hide. Is that your plan? Sit in the dark and rot away while your mom works her butt off? You make me want to puke."

I'd had enough. I lunged forward and shoved Malcolm with both hands. He staggered back, crashing into a chair. "You don't know anything," I said.

He stepped toward me, like one of those damn clown

dolls that bounce up when you punch them down. "Sure. Nobody knows anything but you. Poor Chad. Life is so rough for him. Everyone else gets all the breaks. Let's feel sorry for poor little Chad."

"Shut up." I pushed him again. He stumbled against the table, sending it into the wall with a hollow boom. "My whole life sucks!" I shouted. "My best friend is dying. You understand?" Once I started, it spilled free. "The only girl I ever cared about is going around with a druggie because I didn't have the guts to ask her out. I've got nothing ahead of me. It's all a big zero."

"Well, boo, hoo." He wiped at an imaginary tear.

I swore and threw a punch at his head, but he shot up his left hand and grabbed my wrist.

I let out a scream of rage and frustration as I swung with my free hand, hoping to smash his stupid face. Knock his teeth out. Break his nose. But he grabbed that hand, too, and whipped me around, slamming me into the wall so hard a picture fell down. He stepped forward, pinning my arms against the wall on either side of me.

"You've got so much," he said. "You don't have a clue. And you're just giving up on all of it. Your mother deserves better."

"Leave her out of it!" I rammed my knee up, catching him in the crotch. It wasn't a solid shot, but it was enough to hurt him. His hands dropped from my wrists and he bent down. I pushed his shoulders as hard as I could. He toppled over a chair. "Stay away from her." I rushed toward him.

He rolled to a crouch and tackled me. His shoulder jammed into my gut, knocking the air from my lungs. We crashed to the ground, him on top. I started swearing, spewing out a stream of filth I didn't know was in me. I wanted to kill him. I wanted to stomp him under my feet until every bone in his body snapped.

He slapped me hard enough to shut my mouth, then grabbed my shirt with both fists. The taste of blood bittered my tongue.

I swore. He slapped me again. I didn't care.

"Stay away from my mom," I warned him.

"Listen, you little piece of garbage. Your mother is about the nicest person I've met since I got here. But I'm not interested in her. Not that way. I'm not interested in anyone."

He stood up, lifting me from the floor. I heard a rip as my shirt tore in the back.

"I had a wife. I had a son. They're dead." He shot his arms out, tossing me across the room. My legs hit the couch and I rolled over it, smacking into the wall as I tumbled to the floor. Chips of plaster showered down around me.

Malcolm crossed the space between us and stood over me. "Dead. Gone. So don't tell me your troubles. Your friend's still alive, right?"

I didn't answer. The image of Malcolm as a husband, as a father, stole my voice.

He leaned over and shouted in my face. *"Right?"*

I nodded.

"This girl. This little case of puppy love that you think is the end of the world. Is she dead? Are her ashes scattered at sea? Is she dead?"

I shook my head.

"Then get the hell off your sorry little ass and get back into the world."

He moved away from me to the other side of the couch and stood there, panting. A moment passed. He looked around the room. I sat up and looked, too. It wouldn't have been much worse if a tornado had swept through.

"So," he asked, "you interested?"

"What?"

"The tank, you moron. Yes or no?"

He had to be kidding. He barges in, slaps me around, wrecks the place, calls me names, and wants to know if we can be pals?

I didn't say anything. But I was silent for another reason. Something inside me had changed, and I was only now aware of it. In the fury, in the rage, part of the gray world had burned away. Part of the shroud had fallen loose.

28

I CLIMBED BACK OVER THE COUCH, WINCING AS A BURST OF pain shot through my shoulder.

"Wait right here," Malcolm said. He opened the door and rushed outside. I heard his footsteps travel up the stairs and then across the room above me, followed by the rasping sound of sliding boxes. After a brief silence I heard the clatter of a bunch of small stuff tumbling to the floor. Then more steps, returning. Malcolm dashed back in and dumped an armload of junk on the table. I stared at the pile. Videotapes. And some books.

"Study these, for starters," he said. "The Bozo is just another role. You need to find your interpretation of the part. That's the key." He headed toward the door, then glanced back. "Want help with the couch?"

I shook my head.

"Let me know when you're done with those. I've got plenty more. Remember, we've only got three weeks." He walked out, closing the door behind him.

I managed to tip the couch back, then straightened up the mess. When I finished, I stepped outside. For the first time in ages I felt sunlight on my skin. In my mind I saw myself as an insect that had been dormant in some dark place for eons and was now unfolding shaky legs to join the daylight world. Emerging. The wood on the porch felt rough and sandy beneath my bare feet.

Life still sucked, but one thing had changed. I realized I had a choice. I could roll over and die. Or I could fight back. I had a second chance to do what I should have done in the first place. I took a deep breath of the oven-warm air. Did I have the strength? Was it worth it? I wasn't sure. But I wouldn't know unless I tried.

Everything I wanted was out there. But it all had a price. I could see Gwen, but I'd have to deal with the fact that she liked Anthony. I could go into the dunk tank, but I'd have to do it Malcolm's way. I could be with Jason, but I'd have to accept what was happening to him, however unacceptable it felt.

I went inside and checked out the stack of videos and books Malcolm had dumped on the table. Most of the movies looked like old comedies. There were a bunch of people I'd heard of but not really seen—W. C. Fields, Groucho Marx, and others. And some people I knew, like Robin Williams, Eddie Murphy, and Adam Sandler. I grabbed a couple of the old comedies. I still wasn't sure I wanted anything to do with Malcolm or his movies, but I figured it wouldn't hurt to take some with me to the hospital when I went to see Jason. I owed him a visit. I owed him big-time.

On the way out I spotted a sheet of paper in the corner behind the television. It looked like a printout from a webpage. Probably something Corey had brought over.

At the top, it said, "Wexler-Schiff Antibody Syndrome." Below that, in smaller letters, it said, "A chronic, progressive autoimmune disorder." That sounded bad. That sounded like Jason was going to get sicker and sicker.

There wasn't much information. It was a rare disease. About one case for every half million people in the country. It "tended to affect males of northern European ancestry" and usually showed up anywhere from the age of twelve to sixteen. Sometimes it started in the lungs. Other times it began by paralyzing the vocal chords. I guess Jason was lucky it hadn't taken his voice away. There were some experiments with new treatments, but there wasn't any cure yet. This thing made it sound like there was no hope. That *had* to be wrong.

I crumpled up the page, tossed it in the trash, and headed to the hospital.

"Miss me?" I asked when I stuck my head into Jason's room.

He didn't answer, so I figured he was pissed. I couldn't blame him. I'd abandoned my best friend when he'd needed me. Well, if he was pissed, I'd just have to deal with it. I walked over to the bed. A moment later he opened his eyes halfway. "Chad. Hi."

I felt this awful pressure in my face, like tears were trying to burst free. I glanced toward the hall and thought about running out, then forced myself to turn back. Jason looked way worse than the last time I'd seen him. He'd lost so much weight that his cheekbones cast shadows across his face. His eyes were flat and dull. I wasn't even sure he knew I'd been away.

"How you feeling?" I asked. Man, what a stupid question.

He shrugged.

"Getting a lot of visitors?" I checked the wall. There were no new cards since my last visit. The balloon sagged on a drooping ribbon, its silver skin puckered and loose.

"Some."

This wasn't going well. I was glad to see that the cart with the VCR was still there. "I brought some movies," I told him, holding up the tapes. "Want to watch one?"

He nodded.

I raised the head of the bed. "How's that?"

He nodded again, looking so old and weak that I pretended to study the movie boxes, just to give my eyes somewhere safe to rest. This wasn't Jason. This was Jason's ghost.

I picked a film called *Horse Feathers* and loaded it into the VCR. It was ancient, and it wasn't in color. But it was hilarious. The guy, Groucho Marx—he's the one everyone imitates now with the glasses, mustache, big eyebrows, and cigar—was insanely funny.

"Reminds me of you," I said to Jason after Groucho had gone off on a particularly silly rant. Actually, that wasn't quite true, since Groucho had a harsh edge to his humor. Jason could be wild and crazy. Groucho was wild, crazy, and brutal. But Jason smiled at my comment. It was obvious he was enjoying the movie.

"Another?" I asked after *Horse Feathers* was done.

"Sure," Jason said. "That'd be nice."

I popped in one called *You Can't Cheat an Honest Man*. This had W. C. Fields, the guy with the big nose and the funny voice. It was great. For a while, as I watched the movie, I actually forgot how awful things were. If this was all it took to get a shot at the tank, I guess I could do things Malcolm's way.

Jason started laughing, too. Not much. He didn't have the breath for it. But he laughed. Then, toward the end of the movie, his laughed turned into a cough. His body doubled over as the coughs got worse.

"You okay?" I wondered whether I should call a nurse.

"What are you doing to him?" Jason's mom stormed into the room and switched off the monitor, pushing the button so hard that the whole cart rocked against the wall. "I thought we'd gotten rid of you."

"We were just watching a movie," I said.

She rushed over to Jason and patted him on the back as the coughs shook his whole body. "Don't you ever think?" she asked. "Can't you see he needs to rest? He'll never get better if he doesn't rest."

"But—"

"And you call yourself his friend."

"Sorry." I ejected the movie and gathered up the rest of the tapes.

Jason had stopped coughing. He lay back with his eyes closed, breathing in jerking gasps.

"See you," I said.

He opened his eyes. "Come back and visit me tomorrow, Chad. Okay?"

His mother glared at me. I glanced from her face to his. "I don't know . . ."

"Please."

"Sure." I hurried from the room. This sucked. She'd never stop blaming me. No matter what I did, she'd find something to get mad about. It wasn't my fault he'd started coughing. I was so angry that I was halfway home before the important part sunk in.

Come back and visit me tomorrow, Chad. Okay? That was the longest thing I could remember Jason saying all morning. My visit had been good for him. Maybe he needed a friend nearby to help him get better.

Then the words on that sheet of paper came back to me. *Chronic, progressive . . .* He's not supposed to get better. *Give it up. You can't help.* I forced those thoughts from my mind as I walked the rest of the way home.

Except for the part where Jason's mom had tossed me out, I figured my first attempt to return to the real world had gone okay. I was beat, though. I felt like I'd been working on a roof all afternoon. As much as I wanted to go see Gwen, I'd had enough for one day. I knew I was still traveling along the edge of a cliff. Or maybe the edge of a razor. If I went to the Cat-a-Pult and saw Anthony hanging around with her, or hanging on to her, I was afraid it would blow me so far away, so deep into the gray world, I'd never find my way back.

I didn't want to spend too much time indoors right now, so I dropped off the tapes and put on my cutoffs. Before I left for the beach I grabbed a couple of Malcolm's books. I was curious to see whether they were as good as the movies.

Ellie was at her post. I went over to the lifeguard chair and said hi to her.

"Nice to see you," she said.

"Nice to be here."

That's what I liked about Ellie. She didn't make a big deal over things. And she didn't make me feel guilty about running away from the world.

"Been to the hospital?" she asked.

I nodded. "I was just there."

Something passed between us, like a conversation from my eyes to hers and back. *It's bad. Yeah, it's real bad. Let's not talk about it right now. Let's deal with it later.*

We talked about other stuff for a couple minutes. Then I found a spot on the beach, spread my towel, and stretched out with my eyes closed and my face tilted toward the sun. After a while I rolled onto my stomach and picked up one of the books. It was about acting, and it was way over my head. The first chapter covered all this stuff like motivation and rhythm. I closed that book and tried another.

This one was a lot easier to get into. It was called *Rapier Wits: An Account of Famous Minds at Their Sharpest*. It took me a moment to remember that a rapier was a kind of sword. Buried behind that fancy title, I discovered a book of insults. It had examples of putdowns that all sorts of famous people were supposed to have said. I found a couple that reminded me of lines Malcolm had used in the tank.

There was this one guy, Winston Churchill, who was England's prime minister during World War II. He must have been great to hang out with—as long as you were on his side. He sliced people up with his tongue like it was a sword. According to the book, a woman at this dinner party gave him a hard time about drinking. She'd said, "You, sir, are drunk." He'd shot right back with, "And you, madam, are ugly. But tomorrow I'll be sober." I remembered the first time I'd heard Malcolm. He'd used a version of that in the tank. *I'm wet, but you're funny looking.* Another time, someone had said to Churchill, "If you were my husband, I'd put poison in your tea." He'd told her, "If you were my wife, I'd drink it."

I understood why Malcolm wanted me to read the book. He didn't use the exact words from it, but he'd taken what was in there and built up a supply of ideas. It was like learning to be a better ballplayer by watching the way the best players moved. Whatever reason Malcolm had for loaning me *Rapier Wits,* I wanted to share the book with Jason. He might complain about the Bozo being cruel, but he'd laugh just as hard as the next guy at a good insult.

At five thirty the lifeguards quit for the day. People can keep swimming, but nobody's going to notice if they go under. At six, after she was finished with her work in the lifeguard shack, Ellie came over and plopped down on a corner of my towel.

"What are you reading?" she asked.

I showed her the cover and said, "Insults."

"Why?"

"Research." I grinned, then shared one of the Churchill quotes.

Ellie sighed. "I guess it beats spending all day lying on a couch in a dark room."

"Big-time," I said.

She patted me on the leg as she stood back up. "Well, I'm glad you're back among the living. It wouldn't be summer without you."

"Hey . . ." I said as she started to walk off.

"What?"

"Can you think of any reason a girl wouldn't go out with me?"

"Who?"

"Just someone."

She shook her head. "No reason at all. Want me to put in a good word for you with any particular someone?"

"No. That's okay. Thanks."

I watched her walk off. It was funny. Ellie was pretty and smart, and fun to be with, but I'd never even thought about dating her. I mean, we went out for pizza with the gang, but I didn't want to kiss her any more than I'd want to kiss Jason or Mike or Corey. It was another mystery in a life filled with stuff that just happened, or just didn't happen. I think you can go crazy if you try to find reasons for everything.

I stayed on the beach while the sun set behind me, then watched as the stars came out. By then I was almost alone. They closed the beach at ten, but nobody cared if you were out after that as long as you weren't making trouble. The rule was mostly to keep kids from partying there at night. Couples went for walks all the time. And people surf fished. But a little after ten I started to think about leaving. I figured with my luck I'd be the one they caught when they decided to enforce the regulations. The last thing I wanted was more trouble with the cops. I'd already seen enough blue uniforms to last a lifetime.

After shaking out my towel, I headed home. I didn't bother putting my sandals back on. The sand was cool now and felt good against my feet. The scattered small pinches from broken bits of clamshells didn't bother me.

When I reached my house, I realized I still didn't want to go inside. I'd spent enough time in my cave during the last few weeks. But I didn't feel like wandering around the boardwalk either. Not yet. I knew too many people up there, and some of them would ask where I'd been. I didn't want to get into it. What could I say. I've been away? I went on a mind trip?

Above me, I heard a door open and close, followed by the creak of porch boards.

29

"READ ANY GOOD BOOKS LATELY?" MALCOLM STOOD ON THE upstairs porch, running a towel through his hair. I figured he'd just gotten off his shift and headed right for the shower. I stared at him, trying to sort through the feelings that jumbled around in my mind. I hated his guts. But I also sort of liked him. And that made me hate him even more. On top of all that, he'd briefly opened a window to his past. No. Not a window. It was more like a furnace door. *I had a wife. I had a son.* I was still wrestling with that information.

"You can come up if you promise not to kick me in the balls again," he said.

I joined him on the porch, leaving the insult book down by my door. I wanted to hang on to it for a while. But I brought back the acting book. "This one sucks," I said.

"You're welcome."

"That insult one is pretty good."

"Glad it meets with your approval."

"Sorry about nailing you with my knee," I said.

"That's okay. I've been hit harder. Sorry about slapping you."

"That's okay. I've been slapped harder. Of course, that was by a three-year-old girl."

Malcolm grinned. "Not bad, for an amateur. Did you watch any of the movies?"

"Yup." I told him which ones I'd seen. "They're funny. But I don't need to watch all of them. I'm ready."

"You think just any Bozo can hop in that tank?"

"I could," I said.

"Really?"

"Sure." I didn't see any reason why not. "It's easy."

"Okay." Malcolm pointed down to the street. "Here comes a mark. Let's see you hook him."

"Right now?" I asked. The guy Malcolm picked out looked like he lifted weights—maybe small cars. "Here?"

Malcolm nodded. "Here and now."

"No way. I don't want him punching me out. Why do you think there are bars on the tank?" I could just imagine the guy racing up from the street and chucking me off the porch because I yelled insults at him. I've never backed away from a fight, but I preferred to tangle with opponents who didn't look like they belonged to a different branch of the animal kingdom.

"So speak softly," Malcolm told me. "Keep your voice down. He doesn't have to hear you. This is just practice. Come on, wonderboy. Show me how good you are. Open your mouth. Let the brilliance flow. Amaze me."

"Hey, you," I said as the guy walked past the front of the house. I kept my voice soft enough so it wouldn't reach him. "Are those muscles, or are you carrying a bag of vegetables?"

Not bad, I told myself, though it felt kind of weird talking to a stranger this way—even if he couldn't hear me. I glanced over at Malcolm.

"See? I can do it."

He stared back at me without saying anything, but I could tell from his expression that he wasn't impressed. As I thought about it, neither was I. Maybe I should have said *melons* instead of *vegetables*. No, that wasn't much better. I took another shot. "Hey, muscleboy . . ." In my head, I ran through everything I could think of about weightlifting, trying to find the perfect line. None of it seemed funny.

"Hurry up," Malcolm said.

"Shut up. I'm trying to think." A jumble of bad ideas filled my brain.

"He's getting away. If you let him go, you've lost a mark. No mark, no money. There's nothing sadder than a broke Bozo."

I opened my mouth. But I didn't have anything to say.

"Too late," Malcolm said. "He's gone. Wave bye-bye to him and his wallet."

"Come on, that wasn't fair," I said. "You can't expect me to dream up something just like that."

"Yeah, sure," Malcolm said. "That would be too hard. Nobody could do that." He turned from me and stared out at the street. There was no one in front of us now, but he acted like he was talking to the weightlifter.

"Hey, strongman. You look like you can lift anything. Except your IQ. It must be tough to tell yourself apart from the dumbbells." He threw in a quiet version of his Bozo laugh for good measure.

"Okay, so you knew a couple lines," I said.

But he didn't stop with a couple. "Man, you're strong—maybe you should take a bath. Hey, you must be a body builder—there's no way nature could turn out something that strange on her own. Wow, where'd you get that body? I didn't know they made 'em without a neck. You're looking swell. Or maybe swollen. Better stop before you pop."

He went on for at least five minutes. Finally, as a small group of adults headed down the street in our direction, Malcolm looked at me and said, "Your turn. This is easy. You've got a choice. Take your pick."

"Sure. Just stop talking. You're distracting me."

"Right. Sorry. My mistake. You're absolutely right. There won't be any distractions on the boardwalk. It's such a nice, quiet place to work. So peaceful. Sometimes I like to bring the crossword puzzle with me for that very reason. When it gets really quiet, I meditate."

"Shut up." I wished I'd hit him a whole lot harder this morning.

"My pleasure."

Okay. I'd show him. I scanned the group, looking for the best mark. One of the guys was tall, but not real tall. One of the women was wearing high heels. That's kind of stupid near the beach and boardwalk. But not stupid enough to be worth mentioning. There had to be something I could pick out. That's it—one of the guys had on really baggy pants. "Hey, you," I said, "those pants are so baggy . . . they should . . ." Oh god, I sounded just like Waldo.

My brain switched off again. I sighed and watched as the group walked up the next block. This really wasn't a fair test. I had to worry about keeping my voice down. And they were farther away than they'd be on the boardwalk— all the way down by the street.

"There they go," Malcolm said. "They're spending all their money somewhere else. Tossing dull darts at underinflated balloons or shooting basketballs at microscopic hoops. Apparently, your mime act didn't hold their interest. On the positive side, you're still dry. Congratulations. You could be the world's first waterproof Bozo."

"Okay, you're right!" I shouted. I felt like letting him have it with my knee again. "You're absolutely right. I suck. Thanks so much for proving it." I stormed down the stairs.

"Oh, come now, Chad," Malcolm called after me in a voice like Goofy from the Disney cartoons. "Don't be such a bad sport. Come on back and play."

As I reached the bottom of the steps, I heard him following me. When he was halfway down, he jumped over the railing. I guess he wanted to show off and land right in front of me, but his left leg—the one he limped on—buckled when he hit the ground. He winced in pain, then swore.

"You all right?" I asked.

He nodded. "That was stupid." He held on to the railing and lifted his leg so his injured foot dangled above the ground. For a moment, he closed his eyes and gritted his teeth.

Some of my own anger faded. "You sure you're okay?" I wondered how much of his pain was from the memory of past injuries.

"Yeah. I'll be fine. I just have to avoid leaping off stairs." He leaned against the railing and wrapped his arm around it. "Look, I wasn't trying to prove to you that you suck. Almost everyone sucks at new stuff. Otherwise, we wouldn't need any teachers. I was only trying to prove that you've got a few things to learn before you climb into the tank. You're not so thickheaded that you won't admit that, are you?"

I shrugged, which was the best way I could find to avoid admitting anything.

"Everything looks easy from the outside. Ice-skating looks easy when I see it on television. If I tried to do a triple loop without training, I'd end up flat on my back. Brain surgery looks simple. Maybe I'll go out and saw open someone's skull. Dig around a bit in the cerebellum. How hard could it be?"

"Okay. I get the point. But I figured I could do it. The stuff you say in the tank—I have stuff like that running through my mind all the time."

Malcolm nodded. "Sure, you can be funny. So can I. But that's not good enough. You want to sit in the tank like Waldo and use the same old lame stuff all the time? Waldo's a great guy. I like him a lot. But you and I both know he stinks as a Bozo. Right?"

"Yeah." I had to agree with him on that.

"When Waldo gets in the tank, he's still Waldo. That doesn't work. Nobody wants to dunk Waldo or Malcolm or Chad. You have to be the Bozo. Think of it as a role. A part in a play."

I nodded. That kind of made sense.

"I know you've got dreams of leaping into the tank and being brilliant. But it doesn't work that way. You've got to make some effort. I'm going to ask you just one question. Okay?"

"Sure."

"How badly do you want it?"

"I don't know."

"Not good enough. You have to know. You have to decide whether you're willing to work for it. And before you decide, let me point out that you're a complete idiot for wanting to do this. It's a job nobody is going to appreciate. Yeah, people will laugh when they walk by and maybe notice how clever you are. Even so, they'll think you're nothing but a loser who can't find anything better to do than sit on a ledge waiting to get dunked. Maybe one person in a million will hear you and actually understand what it takes to do the job. And that person will probably be some annoying kid with dreams of glory. Still want it? Or would you be happier if you forgot the whole thing?"

I thought back to the first time I'd seen him in the tank. I remembered how he'd played the crowd like a puppet master. Nobody ignored him. It was impossible to walk past him without stopping, without listening. He had total control. And I thought about the shiver that ran through me when I heard that voice. "I want it."

"Bad enough to work for it?"

"Yeah."

"Okay. Then, for starters, you need to be around the tank as much as possible. I'll tell Bob you'd like your job back."

"But—" I groaned at the thought of gathering balls again.

"See you around seven." Malcolm limped over to the stairs and hobbled up to the porch. As he reached the top, he looked down and told me which movie to study next.

I went inside and watched the movie, keeping the volume low so I wouldn't wake Mom. It was an old film called *Beetlejuice,* about this really whacked-out ghost. I think it was the same guy who played Batman. As I watched, I realized that this was where Malcolm had gotten some of his

Bozo routine. The voice he used was definitely inspired by Beetlejuice. Not completely. But there was an obvious influence.

I set the clock to wake me early so I could visit Jason. He needed to believe there was hope, and I needed to act like he'd leave the hospital someday. That wasn't going to be easy.

I glanced up at the ceiling. Malcolm didn't realize I was already getting a chance to play a role.

I BROUGHT THE INSULT BOOK AND THREE VIDEOS TO THE hospital with me the next morning. I figured Jason's mom would probably come around on her lunch break. I wanted to spend as much time as possible with Jason before then, so I got there at eight.

He was awake when I reached his room. He looked about the same. Still hooked up to tubes. Still no sign that he'd ever be well enough to go home. I sat down and opened up the book.

"Bedtime story?" he asked.

"Better." I read him some of my favorites parts, including all the quotes from Churchill.

He kept telling me they were awful. And he kept telling me they were mean and cruel. But he also kept laughing. I had to stop pretty often. Any time he laughed too hard, he started coughing. At least twice a nurse peered in through the doorway and gave me a suspicious look, like I was doing something wrong. I guess they weren't used to hearing laughter around here. But I didn't get kicked out.

After I'd read him all the best lines in the book, we watched two of the movies. They were both pretty short, but it was getting near lunchtime, so I switched off the monitor. I didn't want Jason's mother catching us. I put the third movie in the VCR, but shut off the power and handed Jason the remote.

"Here. You can watch one after lunch if you feel like it." I'd picked out a tape that looked especially good.

"Thanks. Maybe I will."

"How do you feel?" I was almost afraid to ask that question.

"Tired."

I'd been hoping he'd say he felt better. It seemed like the movies helped. But maybe all they did was take his mind off his problems for a while. And the way he kept coughing, I wondered whether I was hurting him more than I was helping him. Maybe his mom was right.

"I guess I should get going. Need anything?"

He shook his head. "I'm fine."

I headed out. I thought about facing the boardwalk, and the people on the boardwalk, but I still didn't feel ready. Maybe tomorrow.

I spent the afternoon at the beach.

I went home early so I could see Mom before she drove off to school. She was studying when I came in. She must have been surprised that I'd started going out again, but she didn't make a big deal out of it.

"Did you have a good day?" she asked.

"I saw Jason. Then I hung around the beach."

"The beach is nice. I'm glad you got some fresh air. How's Jason doing?" she asked.

"About the same. I don't know if he's ever going to get better."

"You can't give up hope," Mom said. "Jason's a fighter."

"Yeah, he's tough." That sounded so shallow, like a get-well card. *Don't give up. Stay tough. Keep on fighting.* I dug for something positive to say but found nothing. Mom was quiet, too.

Finally, I pointed at the ceiling. "He ever tell you anything about himself?"

She shook her head. "Some people don't share their pain. Professor Vale puts on a good show, but he's carrying a lot of hurt."

That surprised me. Mom was a better judge of people than I'd thought. I never would have guessed that Malcolm had suffered a tragedy, but Mom seemed to know. I wondered if she could see the things that were hidden inside of me.

I shut up and let her get back to studying. After she left for school, I watched another movie. Then, around six thirty, I set out for the dunk tank, taking Gull Avenue, which runs parallel to the shore a block away. For the most part it's just houses and a couple small stores. I cut over to the boardwalk when I got near Wild Willy's Pier, wondering if I really had the job back.

"Hey, there you are," Bob said, as if I hadn't disappeared for a while. He waved at me with the pretzel he was holding, throwing a small spray of mustard, then nodded toward the bucket. "Get to work."

I grabbed the bucket and towel. Another Bozo was just getting ready to leave. Malcolm stepped from the dressing room and motioned for me to join him as he walked toward the tank. I noticed he was limping pretty badly. "Pay attention to everything," he said. "Understand? Study the crowd. Try to guess who I'll pick next. Try to figure out what you'd say."

"Okay."

"There'll be a quiz afterward."

"What?"

"Just kidding." When he reached the tank, he said, "Who am I?"

"Malcolm," I answered without thinking.

He shook his head and pointed at the tank. "Who am I?"

I touched one of the cold steel bars and thought about climbing onto the ledge. "The Bozo?" I guessed.

"Right. Once I get in there, I'm not Malcolm. I'm the Bozo. A bottomless well of venom. Everyone's worst nightmare. The guy you'd love to get even with. I'm the boss who yelled at you today, the teacher who flunked you, the parent who grounded you last week, the bully who stole your lunch money. I'm whoever they need me to be." He grinned and let out one of his patented laughs. "Now get to work."

I took advantage of the changing of the Bozos to gather most of the balls. Then things got busy. While I hustled, I listened to Malcolm and tried to learn as much as I could about the way he worked.

It didn't take long to figure out that each group had a leader—someone who did most of the talking or stood out in some way. Someone who had the ideas and made the choices. Small group, large group, it didn't matter. They all had a leader. And the leader had the most to lose if the group laughed. That made him—or her—the perfect mark.

I thought about our group. No doubt who the leader was. What would happen to us now? I tried not to let my mind go in that direction. Between chasing the balls, listening to Malcolm, and watching the crowd, I almost managed to keep those unhappy images under control.

Around ten Bob handed me a ketchup-smeared twenty-dollar bill and told me I could knock off. But I hung out for another hour, watching and listening while Malcolm finished his shift. Then he climbed out of the tank and Bob closed up for the night. I guess neither of them felt like spending time working the thinning crowds and stragglers at the far end of the day.

"Four hours is pushing it," Malcolm said when he came out of the dressing room. "Three is better. I try to knock off by ten unless the action is just too good. If it's really slow, I might even knock off at nine. The funny thing is, the guys who stink can work all day. They're so mechanical about it, they're like machines. I've seen the truly untalented go for eight hours at a stretch. But I'm shot after four. So, did you learn anything?"

"Pick out the leader. Right?"

"You got it." He looked around, then said, "I'm too wired to go home yet. Want to get some pizza?"

"Sure. You like Salvatore's?"

He nodded, and we headed that way. It immediately felt weird. I should be going there with Jason. I glanced at Malcolm as he limped along next to me. "You sure you want to walk that far?"

"I'm fine."

"How'd you hurt your leg?" I asked. "I mean, the first time. Not last night." The moment the words left my mouth, I remembered what Mom had said. *Some people don't share their pain.* I realized I should mind my own business.

It was a while before he spoke. "Car accident."

Two words that revealed everything. I could tell from his voice that he didn't want to share any details.

As we got near the Cat-a-Pult, I saw them—Anthony and Gwen. She was working. He was waiting. "Crap," I muttered.

"Problem?" Malcolm asked.

"Nothing."

"Must be something. Go on . . ."

"There's this girl."

"That explains it," Malcolm said.

I waited for him to make a joke, but he didn't. After a while, I told him, "She likes this other guy. He's bad news."

"So get off the couch," Malcolm said.

"What?"

"Just because you finally left your little cave doesn't mean you've gotten off the couch yet. Stop being such a lump. Do something. Win her away from him. Be more charming. That can't be hard. Or be tougher. Kick the jerk's butt. Ram your knee into his crotch. I know for a fact you're good at that. Go ahead. Go back and pummel him into the ground—I'll wait."

"Right. And get arrested." If I thought it would work, I'd tackle Anthony right now. But Gwen wasn't the kind of girl who would be impressed by a fistfight.

"I'll tell you what," Malcolm said. His voice got soft and gravelly. "I got a friend named Tommy the Butcher. For a small fee he can break this kid's kneecaps. You'll owe him a favor, of course. To be collected at some later time. One kneecap—small favor. Two kneecaps—big favor. Three kneecaps—trade up for a really big favor."

"Cut it out." I wasn't in the mood for jokes. Though I had to admit the idea appealed to me.

"Get off the couch," Malcolm said again.

I'm trying, I thought, but I didn't bother telling him. "What about you?" I asked when we reached Salvatore's. "You're all hot on acting. Why aren't you out looking for a movie or a play to be in?"

He didn't answer. I got lost in my own thoughts, wondering whether there really was something I could do to get Gwen away from Anthony. Nothing brilliant came to mind. Though a lot of violent things did. We bought slices to go and walked back.

"See you tomorrow," I said to Malcolm when we reached the house.

As he climbed up the steps, he looked down at me and said, "I'd make a great Hamlet, wouldn't I? Limping across the stage, hobbling through the sword fights. Very impressive."

"What?"

"Nobody in Hollywood will hire an actress who has even one little pimple. How much work do you think there is for a guy who walks like a lab assistant from a grade B horror film? I can just see the reviews. *While the rest of the cast was stunning, Malcolm Vale turned in another lame performance.*" He went on up to his door and vanished inside.

I hadn't thought about that. He was right. A blemish was rare in Hollywood. Anything more noticeable was left for bad guys, sidekicks, and Clearasil commercials. But there still had to be lots of acting jobs out there. Especially for someone with his talent. And except when he hurt himself, his limp wasn't really all that noticeable. *How badly do you want it?* Maybe I'd stumbled on the truth about Malcolm—he wasn't ready to get off the couch *he* had crawled onto.

He'd lost his whole family. I couldn't imagine what that was like. I might have lost a father, but that was different. At least I had one good parent.

I thought about Gwen. Can you lose what you never had? And about Jason. I wasn't going to lose him. No way.

Despite the churning of my mind, I slept well. Those hours at the tank had wiped me out. I guess that was the good thing about hard work.

In the morning I went back to see Jason. No matter what, I was going to visit him every day.

"Bring any more movies?" he asked when I came in.

I held up three tapes. "Sure thing." I dropped down in the chair next to the bed. He looked a little better than yesterday. There was a small touch of color in his face. And he seemed to be breathing easier. Or maybe I was just getting used to seeing him this way. The little changes are hard to notice. I knew if I saw pictures side by side, Jason now and Jason before he got sick, the difference would be awful.

"You watch the one I left?" I asked.

He nodded. "Three times. It was great."

I put in another movie. *Duck Soup.* Groucho Marx again. Jason still couldn't laugh too much without breaking into a coughing fit, so I kept the remote right next to me. But a couple times I got so wrapped up in laughing that I forgot to stop the tape. And I forgot to watch the clock.

So I suppose it was my fault that Jason was in the middle of coughing his head off when his mom burst into the room.

"I warned you about this!" she screamed.

I leaped from my chair and popped out the tape.

"You're trying to kill him. You vicious little bastard! You're trying to kill my son." She picked up a box of tissues and threw them at me. They bounced against my chest and fell to the floor.

Jason was still coughing too much to speak.

"I'm just trying to make him feel better," I said.

"Get out!" she yelled.

I hurried from the room. I was too angry to wait for the elevator, so I raced down four flights of steps and left the hospital. This really sucked. I was only trying to help a friend. And all I got for it was trouble.

"The hell with her," I said, slapping a stop sign with my open palm. "The hell with everything." None of this was worth the abuse.

I could feel the grayness closing back in on me. It would be so easy to give in and give up. Then I wouldn't have to watch Jason withering away while his mother cursed at me. I wouldn't have to deal with cops who blamed me for stuff I didn't do. Cops who acted like I was no better than my dad. I wouldn't have to see Gwen smiling at Anthony. I sped up, eager to get home, where I could draw the curtains and lie in the dark.

To my right, three small children played tag on a lawn, giggling as they chased each other. Ahead, I heard the splash of someone doing a cannonball into a backyard pool. The sun heated my face as I thought about the welcoming grayness.

It was a world without pain.

It was also a world without possibilities. If I went there,

I'd never see Jason laugh. I'd never see Gwen smile at me. I'd never find out what it felt like to lean into that microphone and let loose at the world. And I'd never prove I was better than everyone thought. I'd just be running away. I could hear Mom's words. *You're so much like your father.* No way. Never.

I forced myself to stop walking. I wasn't going back to the couch. I couldn't return to that world. Not while Jason was stuck up there in that room, spending most of the day by himself. Not while everyone else had given up on him and was just waiting for him to die. I turned around and headed back to the hospital.

I hung out behind a tree at the edge of the parking lot, watching for Jason's mom. I knew she blamed me for everything. I realized it looked bad if Jason was coughing his head off every time his mom came to the room. But she was wrong. Dead wrong. I wasn't hurting Jason. I was sure of that, as sure as I'd ever been of anything. I was helping him. Jason had felt better after we'd watched the movies. And after I'd read to him.

As soon as I saw Jason's mom drive off, I went back up to the pediatrics floor. I almost expected to see a poster with my face inside a slashed red circle. But nobody seemed to care whether I was there or not. I guess the nurses had other things to worry about. So I went to Jason's room, ready to start another movie marathon.

But I couldn't. The VCR was gone.

31

"WHAT HAPPENED?" I ASKED.

Jason shrugged. "Mom's idea."

"She had them take it away?" I could just see her wheeling the whole thing out herself, pushing it across the room while the plug ripped from the socket.

"Yeah." He sighed and glanced toward the hall.

"She hates me," I said.

Jason shook his head. "No. She's just upset."

No kidding. "Did you tell her I wasn't doing anything bad?"

"I tried." He coughed a bit, then said, "She'll get over it."

"I hope so." Another worry crossed my mind. Maybe she wasn't the only one who didn't like what I was doing. "You want me here, right?" I asked.

"For sure."

Relieved, I plopped down on the chair and looked around the room. There was still a regular television mounted in the corner opposite the bed. "Want to watch something?" I could tell that Jason was getting worn out from talking.

"Okay."

"Not much on," I said after flipping through the channels. I settled for an old western. I'd hoped to find something funny, but it looked like we were out of luck.

A while later, a nurse walked past the room, carrying a bed pan.

"Check it out," I said, trying to make my voice sound like W. C. Fields from the old movies. "Guess they're making soup in the cafeteria."

It was gross, but Jason laughed. That got me started. "If I were you, I wouldn't eat the pea soup."

He groaned. But then he laughed.

I was on a roll.

"It must be hard to work in that kitchen. I'll bet the chef is pooped."

One idea flowed into another. "Waiter, there's a fly in my soup," I said, talking like someone who's always complaining. I switched to a waiter's voice. "Don't worry, sir, I'll zip it up."

I wiggled my eyebrows like Groucho Marx and said, "This place stinks. People are dying to get out." It was a twist on the old joke about the graveyard—people are dying to get in. But that didn't matter. Jason laughed again.

A doctor went running past. "Poor guy must have lost his patients," I said.

I liked being Groucho, so I stuck with it. For the next hour, I played the part, making ridiculous jokes and tossing out comments about everyone who walked past. Just having fun.

Jason laughed, and he coughed, and he groaned at the bad jokes. Behind me, the western played on unwatched.

Finally, I stopped to catch my breath.

"Man, you're crazy," Jason said. But he was grinning.

"I am," I agreed.

"Pea soup," he said, shaking his head. "Thought I was gonna die."

Thought you were, too. I remembered something our gym teacher used to say. *Whatever doesn't kill you makes you stronger.* Was I killing my best friend, or making him stronger?

Jason was panting, gasping, coughing little coughs, still catching his breath. Still weak and sick. But no doubt about it, he seemed better. I realized I was feeling better, too. My heart ached over Gwen, but maybe it was an ache I could fix. At the very least, it was an ache that would heal. In the meantime I didn't care what Jason's mom did. She could burn all the movies in the world and smash all the VCRs. I was still going to make him laugh. All I needed was my mind and my mouth.

Later that afternoon I went home and watched more movies, memorizing the funniest parts so I could share them with Jason. That evening I listened again to Malcolm while I worked at the Bozo tank. The next morning I went back to see Jason. I told him some of Malcolm's best lines from the night before.

"That's awful," he'd say. Then he'd laugh.

I thought up a new gag. While I talked, I slipped off my chair like I was getting dunked.

Jason enjoyed that, too. "You still want to be a Bozo?" he asked as I got up from the floor.

"Yeah. I must be out of my mind, but I want it as much as . . ." I caught myself. *As much as you want to play volleyball in Santa Monica.* "I just really want to do it."

"Why?"

I searched for words to explain my feelings and wondered whether anyone could give a good answer to that question. Why did Corey want to design websites? Why did Ellie like biology? What makes a kid sit in his room every day practicing guitar chords or painting pictures for hours at a time? What makes a guy spend years chiseling away at a block of marble? Maybe it was just some feeling in the gut that said, *Do this.*

Jason shrugged. "You'd be good. Maybe that's why."

"Thanks." That made as much sense as anything. I guess it was better to be a good Bozo than a bad engineer or lawyer. I slipped off the chair again. It wasn't as funny the second time.

When I ran out of lines from Malcolm, I pretended I was W. C. Fields playing a doctor. "I'd take your temperature," I told Jason, shaking an imaginary thermometer, "but I'm not sure which end smells better."

Then Groucho stopped by, and Beetlejuice, and a dozen others. All during that time, no matter who I was on the outside, on the inside a part of me was thinking about Gwen. But I tried to keep that part separate so it wouldn't cast a shadow over Jason's laughter.

That became my routine. Hospital, home, dunk tank. Day after day. A week passed. Jason wasn't coughing as much. And he seemed to be able to talk a bit more without growing tired. In the middle of the second week, the routine got interrupted. I found Malcolm waiting for me on the porch when I came home from the hospital. "No work tonight," he said.

"What?"

"We're going on a field trip."

32

MALCOLM WOULDN'T TELL ME ANYTHING MORE. A COUPLE minutes later a battered old Lincoln pulled up by the curb.

"Let's go," Malcolm said, hopping in the front passenger side.

"Hello, stranger," Doc said when I got in the backseat. "I thought you'd moved. Or maybe you didn't like me anymore."

"I was dealing with some problems," I told Doc. "Sorta gave up for a while." I figured if there was anyone I could be honest with, it was him. Doc never seemed to judge anyone—as long as you didn't bang on his machines.

He nodded. "Been there myself. Glad you survived."

We took the Parkway north for a couple miles, then cut over inland along one of the local highways. Doc kept up most of the conversation all by himself, telling stories about his own early days traveling the country and doing odd jobs. After half an hour we swung off the highway and drove down the main street of a small town. At the far end of the town, Doc pulled into a crowded parking lot next to a church. Behind the church, in a large field, I saw a Ferris wheel, a couple smaller rides, and a bunch of game booths. The smell of grilled sausages drifted through the open window, along with the sweet, greasy aroma of funnel cakes.

"Sort of a long way to travel to see stuff we can walk to," I said as I searched the small carnival for anything halfway interesting.

Malcolm grinned and got out of the car. "Oh, there's something here we don't have on the boardwalk."

"What?" I asked. "Hand-powered merry-go-rounds?"

"You'll see."

I followed Malcolm and Doc through the parking lot. We passed by the games and the food at the far side of the carnival. Right in the center of the midway, a huge crowd blocked the path. Even before I could see anything, I could hear him.

It was a Bozo.

And he was even better than Malcolm.

"Who is that?" I asked.

"Jordy Ketchum," Doc told me. "One of the best in the business."

"He's a legend," Malcolm said. "Watch and learn."

I worked my way closer. Jordy was amazing. He didn't just taunt the mark. He kept up a steady stream of chatter, involving everyone in the crowd, lining up his next three or four marks ahead of time while he sunk the hook in his latest vic. I watched him snag a man, a woman, and a boy.

"Hey, check out the gut on that guy. Looks like someone pumped him full of air. Don't laugh, lady. I think you're the one they took the air from. Holy cow, kid—if your ears stuck out any farther, you'd have to file a flight plan."

The kid got to the barker first.

"Step right up, kid. That's it. Three for two dollars. Pay the guy with the apron. Try not to hit him with an ear. Give him a ten, you'll get four dollars change. Yeah, kid, listen to me. I give good advice. That's how I ended up in this high place. If you want to be a sport, buy the big guy some food. Looks like he hasn't eaten in at least thirty seconds. How 'bout you, lady? You eat anything this month?"

The kid threw a ball. The skinny woman and the guy with the big stomach lined up for their turns.

"Nice try, kid. This time aim for the target. Give him a hand, folks. He sure could use it. And an arm, too. Just keep your hands away from the big guy. If he gets hungry, you might lose a finger. Haaaaaaa." His laugh was simpler than Malcolm's chain-saw cackle. He didn't need the extra flair.

By the time the kid dunked him, he'd gotten another mark in line with the man and the woman. The action never stopped. He even had priests and nuns chucking balls at the target—all in good fun, of course. Jordy ruled. No question. He was king. The whole time he sat on the ledge in that beat-up old carnival dunk tank, he was the center of the universe. Finally, over protests from the crowd, he took a break and ducked into a tent.

"This way." Malcolm led me over there.

"Hey, Barrymore," Jordy said when we walked in. He was sitting on, and dripping into, a large easy chair. "Good to see you." He leaned forward and shook hands with Malcolm.

I gave Doc a puzzled look. "Barrymore?"

"Nickname," he explained. "Famous actor from before your time. Drew's granddaddy."

Malcolm and Jordy exchanged greetings. "Hey, Slim," Jordy said when he caught sight of Doc. I guess he had a nickname for everyone.

"Were you ever skinny?" I asked Doc.

He snorted. "I was born fat. Jordy likes irony."

They introduced me, but they were so wrapped up in reliving the old days that I just stood off to the side and listened. Close up, even with his makeup on, I could tell that Jordy must have been at least as old as the bank robber I'd met in jail. I wondered whether he had any plans to retire. Did Bozos ever quit? Or did they just slowly dissolve?

"Chad wants to be a Bozo," Malcolm told Jordy at one point.

Jordy glanced over at me. "Is that the truth?"

I nodded.

"Hey, I wanted to be a veterinarian," Jordy said. "And look where I ended up. You never know, kid. You never know." He laughed and returned to his conversation with Doc and Malcolm.

After his break, Jordy headed back out to the tank. "Take care, Chatterbox," he said, winking at me as he walked by. I smiled as I thought about running into him again many years from now. *Hey, Chatterbox. Good to see you. How ya been?*

We stayed until midnight, when the fair closed.

"That," Malcolm said as we pulled out of the parking lot, "is pure genius. You can't buy talent like that."

I nodded. "Pretty awesome."

"A lot of carnival Bozos don't even hook the marks," Doc said. "They'll just wait for someone to step up, and then go into a routine. Not Jordy. He's a master."

"I learned a lot from him," Malcolm said. He shook his head. "I was in bad shape when we met. Bad time in my life. He helped me out." Malcolm didn't give any details, but I had a good idea what he was talking about.

We rode the rest of the way back pretty much in silence. When we reached the house, I thanked Doc for taking me, then stepped out to the curb.

"Want to practice for a little while?" Malcolm asked.

"Sure." I followed him up to the porch and waited for someone to walk past. Even this late, there was always foot traffic. Nobody paid attention to the clock during a vacation. Before long, a guy and his girlfriend strolled down the street in our direction. Inspired by hours of watching Jordy, I came up with a line right away. "Hey mister, don't forget to curb your dog." That would do the trick. She wasn't bad looking, but I figured this was the sort of comment that would force the guy to pay for a chance to dunk me. I grinned at Malcolm.

"No way," he said.

"What?" My grin melted.

"First, that's just plain cruel without being funny. It's something a schoolyard bully would say. Second, you're talking to him but insulting her. Even if he dunks you, she doesn't get the revenge. He ends up feeling proud and macho. She still feels like crap. No good. Understand?"

"Yeah." He was right. It was the sort of line one of the bad Bozos would come up with. The moment I admitted that to myself, my anger faded. I studied the couple as they passed us. The guy was wearing his pants real low. "Hey, nice belt. Wait—that's your stomach. My mistake."

"Better," Malcolm admitted. "Still not great, but better."

"Hey, man, either pull up those pants or get some plaster to fill in your butt crack."

Malcolm roared, causing the couple to glance up at us.

When he caught his breath, he said, "Very funny, Chad. There's just one problem."

"A little too PG for the boardwalk?" I asked.

He nodded. "There are families out there. Lots of little kids. Everything you say is broadcast to all ears, whether they want to hear you or not. Keep it G-rated. Stay away from butt cracks, breasts, and anything else you wouldn't discuss with your mom."

"Farts?" I asked.

"Probably not."

The next mark came into sight, so I got back to work.

After about an hour, Malcolm said, "Had enough?"

"Yeah, I'm beat."

"Let's knock off. Hey, how's your friend?"

"I don't know. They say he's never going to get better, but I don't believe them." I told him that I'd been trying to keep Jason laughing. "Maybe I'm crazy, but I think it's helping him." I realized I sounded like a little kid chattering away about some sort of playground ritual. Or a mark explaining his system for beating the big number wheel.

I didn't expect Malcolm to believe me. But he said, "You're not the first person to notice the connection. Wait here." He ran inside. I could tell from the clunks and crashes that he was digging around for something deep among the boxes. He finally came back with a book and a movie. "Watch this," he said, wiggling the hand that held the movie. "Read this," he said, wiggling the book. "Don't get them mixed up or you'll break your VCR and go blind."

"Thanks." I took them downstairs. The movie, *Patch Adams,* was about a doctor who believed that humor helped people heal. The whole thing was based on a true story. It was late when I turned off the TV and opened the book. The title, *Anatomy of an Illness,* didn't sound very funny, or very interesting. But I ended up reading the whole thing before I went to sleep. It was about a guy who'd cured himself of an incurable disease by laughing. The doctors told him he'd never get better. Like Jason, he had a chronic, progressive disease. Not the same one, but something just as awful. He noticed he felt better after he laughed. So he watched funny movies and tapes of old TV comedy shows and laughed as much as possible. And proved all the doctors were wrong. He did other stuff, too, like take lots of vitamins. But he felt it was the laughter, as much as anything, that made a difference.

I slept until half past noon. As soon as I got up, I headed for the hospital to see Jason. After making sure his mom's car wasn't in the parking lot, I went up to his room.

"How you feeling?" I asked.

"Could be worse. They said my enzyme levels were better."

"That's good, right?"

Jason shrugged. "I guess. The doctor seemed surprised. He came back to see me three times yesterday."

"We're going to surprise him a whole lot more," I told Jason. "We're going to surprise the heck out of him. Out of all of them."

Jason looked puzzled.

I handed him the book Malcolm had given me. "Read this later. Okay?"

"Is it funny?"

I shook my head. "Nope. Dead serious." As much as laughter would help him, I knew it would work even better if he believed in it. That's something else I'd learned from the book. Everything worked better if you believed. That's why a sugar pill could cure a headache if the person thought the pill was medicine, or why a witch doctor's spell could kill someone who thought the power was real.

"Promise you'll read it?" I asked.

"Does this look like school?" he asked.

I held out my hand. "One dollar. Pay up."

Jason stuck his hand into the pocket of his pajama top and shrugged. "I owe you one."

"Look. I'm not kidding. You have to read this. Okay?"

"Sure."

"Great." I turned my attention to making Jason laugh. In a way, it still seemed crazy that something like laughter could help. But I'd bet it seemed crazy when a scientist first claimed that mold could cure infections, or that sunlight helped the body make vitamin D. Putting all of that aside, there was something else that made a believer out of me. I knew I felt better when I laughed. It was that simple.

I told Jason about the trip to see Jordy and about the progress I was making in my Bozo training, and I repeated some of the better lines I'd come up with on the porch. Then I checked the television. This time I found a funny movie. "Maybe you can get them to bring back the VCR," I said.

Jason nodded. "I'll try."

I stayed until his dinner came, then headed home. We'd laughed a lot. I felt good. Jason was still real sick. No doubt about it. But there was hope. Maybe he could heal himself. Maybe I could help.

There was another part of my life that needed healing.

An hour or so after I got home, I went to the boardwalk and headed for the Cat-a-Pult.

Gwen was at the booth. Anthony wasn't. I wondered whether they'd broken up. That would be wonderful, but I knew I was fooling myself if I believed my problems had solved themselves while I wasn't looking. There was a big difference between hope and fantasy. I stared at the booth for another moment, remembering what had happened last time I'd been there. I'd left that wound untreated long enough. Telling myself it would be different than before, I went to talk with Gwen.

33

I DIDN'T WAIT FOR HER TO NOTICE ME. I'D SPENT TOO MUCH of my life standing in silence, hoping someone else would speak. "Hi, Gwen," I said as she handed a player his change.

"Oh, hi, Chad." She smiled, but it was a small smile, like the sort you'd share with a stranger.

"How you doing?" I asked.

"Fine." She crossed to the other side of the booth to take care of another player.

I followed her over. "I haven't seen you in a while."

"You haven't been around much," she said.

A dozen replies ran through my mind. *I was keeping a sick friend company.* True, but it made me sound like I was trying to earn points. Look at me—best friend in the world, takes care of the sick and feeds the poor. Saint Chad. Nope. *I've been busy.* That sounded conceited. *I stayed away while my heart mended.* No way.

"Yeah," I said. Man, talk about a meaningless answer. I had to come up with something that at least sounded reasonable. "A lot of stuff's been going on. What've you been up to?"

She shrugged. "Working. Going out."

"With Anthony?" The question came out louder than I'd planned.

She nodded. "He's very nice."

No, he isn't! It's all an act. I wanted to grab her and shake her and shout the truth. *He's bad news. He'll get you in trouble. He might hurt you just for the fun of hurting me.* But anything I said against Anthony would just make me look like a jealous fool. And if I didn't say anything, I'd look like a jerk, too. "I've known him for a while," I muttered.

"He's honest," she said. "He tells me how he feels. Most guys don't do that." Her eyes drilled through me as she spoke those words.

No! He tells you what you want to hear. "Most guys have a hard time saying how they feel." That was so true, but it sounded so lame.

"Most girls don't like trying to read minds," she said.

This was going in the wrong direction. But I wasn't willing to back off. Not until I had a chance to ask her out. "Long shift?"

"Pretty long. I'm here until ten."

Go for it. "So, are you busy after that?"

She nodded. "Yeah."

"Oh." I felt like I was banging on a locked door.

"Anthony's taking me to a party tonight," she said.

"That's nice." Actually, that sucked.

"It's at his brother's house."

"Tommy's place?" Oh, man. Not there. I thought about the rented house on Abbot Drive that Anthony's brother shared with a couple other guys. They were wasted all the time. Everyone around here knew about them.

Let it go. Maybe my life would be better if I just gave up this painful dream. I'd blown my chances in too many ways—by keeping my mouth shut when I should have spoken, and by screaming my head off when I should have kept quiet. But the thought of Gwen partying with that crowd of drugged-out scum made me flinch.

A horrible thought hit me. Was I wrong about her? Was she Anthony's type of girl and not mine? I looked in her eyes, trying to see what was really there. It was no use. I couldn't tell anything that way. I didn't have Mom's gift for peering through masks.

Crap. I didn't need this. I was sick of spending so much of my life inside my head. I was sick of struggling with everything. Even a stupid jellyfish is smart enough not to waste its life battling against the tide. "Have a great time," I said. I sped away, fighting the numbness that tried to seep through my body.

It was close to seven, so I headed over to the Bozo tank. At least work would keep me busy. I ran into Malcolm near the entrance to the pier, standing in line at the NutShack.

"Getting Bob a small snack," he said. "Preferably something sticky. I think it's charming the way he uses condiments to groom his mustache."

"Uh-huh."

"Want something?"

"Nah."

"Hey, cheer up," he said. "You look like your best friend just died."

I stared at him.

"Sorry. Poor choice of words. But you really do look pretty pathetic. I've seen happier faces on roadkill. For that matter, I've seen happier faces on canned hams. What's up?"

I told him about Gwen and the party at the drug house.

"Sounds like a bad place for a nice girl," he said. "Hell, it even sounds like a bad place for a bad girl. I've walked past that part of Abbot Drive. Scary."

I nodded. "Nothing much I can do about it. I blew my chance."

"Sometimes life sucks," Malcolm said as he reached the front of the line. "I don't suppose a candy apple would do much to lift your spirits."

"Thanks anyhow." I waited while he got his order. When he was done, we headed over to the tank.

Malcolm handed Bob a giant hunk of caramel popcorn, then slipped into the dressing room. I got to work, trying to lose myself between the mindless task of gathering the balls and the complex task of learning the craft of the Bozo. My own turn in the cage wasn't far off now. July was almost over. Malcolm said I'd get a shot in early August. The scary thing was that the more I learned, the less ready I felt.

Around nine thirty I spotted Anthony heading past, on his way to the Cat-a-Pult. "Right back," I told Bob.

"Hey, Ballzo," Anthony said when I rushed over to him. "What's up?"

"Don't take Gwen to your brother's place," I said. "She's a nice girl."

"She's very nice," he said. "No point partying with a pig."

He flashed me a smile, then walked away.

If the universe was at all fair, Anthony would drop dead before he took another step. But that wouldn't happen. He'd get whatever he wanted. And the rest of us would get stepped on. For the first time in my life, I really understood how one person could kill another.

As violent fantasies tore through my mind, I went back to work, where I watched other people buy a brief chance to get even with the world. They were lucky. It would take more than a Bozo to make me feel right.

We didn't finish until around eleven. As I was walking toward home with Malcolm, he said, "Hold on. I need to check something." I waited while he made a quick call from one of the pay phones by the information booth.

"Did you read that book?" he asked when he came back.

"Yeah. It's amazing. They told the guy he'd never get better. But he got better."

"You're right—it's amazing. But you can't always count on miracles," Malcolm said. "It's not like we could empty out the hospitals by running continuous Three Stooges film festivals. But it would probably do a lot of good."

"Sometimes there *are* miracles," I said.

"Sometimes you can make your own miracles. It never hurts to try."

"Why don't you come with me to visit Jason tomorrow?" I figured Malcolm could help me to keep him laughing.

"No, thanks. I don't like hospitals."

"Come on. He'd be happy to see you."

Malcolm sighed. "Want me to bring the tank? We can cheer up your friend and make a few bucks."

I realized he was kidding, but the combined images of the dunk tank and the hospital brought up something else I'd been thinking about for a while. "You know what's funny?" I asked.

"I should hope so," he said. "Otherwise, I'd be the world's driest Bozo."

"No, seriously."

"Okay, seriously, what's funny?"

"Laughter can heal, right?"

"Right."

"But it can also hurt."

"You're pretty smart for someone who wants to spend his life dangling over a pool of stagnant water."

"Thanks."

"It's not a simple subject. People far smarter than either of us have written whole books about laughter and comedy," Malcolm said.

"Are they any good?" I asked.

He shook his head. "Boring, for the most part. And, oddly enough, rarely funny."

We took our time going back. I didn't want to walk too fast, since Malcolm was still limping pretty badly. "Jason thinks Bozos are cruel," I said.

"Absolutely."

"You're kidding." I didn't expect Malcolm to agree with that.

"There's no way around it. Cruelty is part of the act. We say nasty things to people. Wrapped up in cleverness. But it's in a controlled situation. Nobody gets hurt. Or at least they don't get hurt in a way that leaves scars. And an opportunity for revenge is a mere two dollars away."

I thought about all the skill he put into his performance. It almost seemed wasted on the marks. "There's so much you could do with your talent," I said.

A long moment passed before Malcolm spoke. "The trouble is, I'm really good at this."

The way he said it, he wasn't boasting—just stating a

fact. He sounded kind of sad about it. Like he was so good he didn't have a choice. I knew kids in school who'd been trapped into playing sports they didn't like just because they had some talent.

"You'll be teaching in the fall, right?" I asked.

"Yeah. Figured I'd try something different. Not sure if I'll like it."

"You've done a good job teaching me," I said. We'd reached the ramp.

"Now don't get all soft and misty on me. I left my Kleenex in my other pants."

"Seriously, you've taught me a lot."

"That remains to be seen."

We headed toward Sea Crest. As we turned the corner, Malcolm said, "She was my high-school sweetheart. It sounds pretty corny, doesn't it?"

I realized he wasn't expecting an answer. I waited for him to go on.

"Linda Beth Cassidy. Libby, to her friends. She was the first girl I ever met who thought my jokes were funny. Her eyes sparkled when she laughed. We kept dating while I went to college. Got married right after I graduated. It was like a dream. I started getting acting work right away. Commercials. Small plays. I was the golden boy. I'd been offered a role in a TV series. We took a vacation to celebrate. Kent, our son, was in the backseat.

"The weather was fine. I wasn't speeding. I was sober." Malcolm shrugged. "A tire blew on the car in front of us. It spun out of control. Eight cars were involved in the crash. Only two people died."

"Oh, man," I whispered.

"One minute I had everything. An instant later I had nothing. I didn't even have someone to blame."

I tried to find the right words. I knew he wouldn't want my pity. *I'm sorry* seemed like too little. Anything more felt like too much. Malcolm saved me from saying something awkward. "You in the mood to practice a bit when we get back?" he asked.

"Sure. No reason not to."

It turned out there was a big reason. As we reached the house, three police cars came screaming up to the curb, sirens howling like tonight was the end of the world.

34

ANOTHER BLUR OF BADGES, BRIGHT LIGHTS, AND BLUE UNIFORMS. "Mom!" I yelled. Something must have happened to her. A thousand fears rolled over me. But she came out of the house and stepped onto the porch as six car doors flew open. A couple cops jogged up the walkway to the house. Another pair rushed toward me and Malcolm. I had this crazy impulse to run. I wanted to vanish into the night. Especially when I saw Costas and Manetti getting out of the third car.

They herded us inside. One of the policemen asked Mom if they could look around. She nodded and mumbled something about having nothing to hide. Officer Manetti explained everything while the rest of the cops searched the house. "We were tipped off to a drug party on Abbot Drive," he told Mom.

At the mention of drugs, Mom's gaze shot in my direction. Her expression twisted with fear.

My own face must have twisted as an awful image exploded in my mind. Gwen in handcuffs, dragged out of the house along with everyone else.

Officer Manetti kept talking. "We arrested a number of people for possession and underage drinking. One of them told us your son was his supplier."

"That's a lie!" I shouted. With a sickening jolt, it all fell into place. I glared at Malcolm, who'd settled down onto the couch. That phone call he'd made—*he* was the one who'd tipped off the cops. And now he was watching everything from his front-row seat, sucking it all in like it was just another scene to add to his collection. Oh, man. Anthony must have thought I was the one who'd ratted him out. He'd given them this story to get even. He probably figured they'd find some kind of drugs when they searched here. Druggies always assumed everyone else was using.

"I didn't do anything," I said, looking toward Mom. She'd fallen into a stunned silence, like a deer dropped in the middle of a busy highway. This was bad, but I knew it wouldn't get any worse. I was clean. No drugs. They could search the house one atom at a time and they wouldn't find anything illegal. "It's okay, Mom. You'll see."

I walked over to Malcolm. "Nice going. You got Gwen in big trouble."

"Or out of big trouble," he said quietly, not even bothering to look at me.

At least I'd be out of trouble soon, too—with the cops, that is. I knew there'd be trouble with Mom when they left.

"Got it!" Costas shouted, stepping back from the closet.

Anger replaced my fear. He was setting me up. If he'd found anything, he'd planted it.

Costas turned around, holding an old shoe box. "Drug money," he said as he dumped the cash onto the table.

Manetti whistled. "Jeez, kid, you make more than I do." He put on a pair of rubber gloves and started counting the money.

I hadn't bothered to keep track of it. I'd just tossed

whatever Bob paid me into the box each night. I tried to guess what was there. I'd worked nearly every day for the last two weeks. Bob usually gave me twenty. Sometimes more. There was money in it from before, too, when I'd been running errands.

"Three hundred and seventy-eight bucks," Manetti said. "Looks like you're going to take a ride, kid. You might as well tell us now. Make it easy on yourself. I'm sure the lab guys will be able to find traces of drugs in here."

"It's not drug money," I said.

Costas laughed. "You must know the world's most generous tooth fairy."

Manetti ignored his partner and asked me, "Then where's it from?"

I looked over at Mom. I was doomed either way. If I admitted I was working at the Bozo tank, she'd know I'd broken my promise. But if I kept quiet, they'd drag me back to jail. It didn't matter that I hadn't done anything. I'd heard plenty of stories about innocent kids who were arrested and ended up spending months in jail before the mistakes got straightened out. The last thing I wanted was to show up on some TV news magazine as an example of how far the system could go wrong. No way I wanted my new best friend to be some guy with a nickname like Killer or Mad Dog.

"I've been working," I said. I glanced at Malcolm, knowing he'd back me up.

But he wouldn't catch my eye. It was like he didn't want anyone to realize he was there.

Oh, my god. Another thought hit me. The cops still believed he was my dad. If he talked with them, they'd say something like *Your son is in a lot of trouble.* Mom would tell them *That's not his father.* Then Malcolm would be screwed. And Mom would find out about my trip to jail.

"Where've you been working?" Manetti asked.

"The dunk tank," I said. I wanted to point to Malcolm and say *Ask him.* So what if he got in trouble? He deserved it for making that phone call. I imagined him sitting in a jail cell. Jumbled images raced through my mind. The cell turned into the dunk tank. I saw him falling again and again while Stinger, dressed as a cop, nailed the target. Then Stinger became Saul, the old bank robber, making conversation. *So, you got a wife? Any kids? Tell me about your family.*

Costas shook his head, as if he didn't believe me. Crap. I realized he'd heard me make the same claim the night on the boardwalk when I was trying to sneak into the tank. He hadn't believed me back then, either. To him, I was just a liar and a thief. And now a drug dealer. "Can you prove it?" he asked.

Not tonight, I thought. The tank was closed. Bob was gone from the boardwalk until tomorrow. I didn't even know how to get in touch with him.

"He works with me," Malcolm told them. He got up and stepped away from the couch. "Our boss is a pig. Check the bills. There'll be ketchup or mustard all over them."

Manetti looked down at the money and then at his gloved hands. "That's disgusting."

Malcolm pulled a card from his wallet. "Here's his name and number. Bob Kirkhaus. It'll check out."

"You'll vouch for your—"

"Absolutely," Malcolm said, cutting Manetti off before he could say the word *son.*

221

"Okay," Manetti said, putting the money back in the box and peeling off the gloves. He took the card from Malcolm, then looked back at me. I noticed that Malcolm had slipped a couple steps away, removing himself from the conversation again.

The other four cops headed out, leaving Costas and Manetti to wrap things up.

"So how does this Anthony know you?" Manetti asked.

"We like the same girl," I told him.

"Isn't she lucky," Costas said with a snort.

I ignored him and asked Manetti, "Did any girls get arrested?"

He nodded. "A couple."

I wanted to ask if one of them was a redhead, but Officer Costas grabbed my shoulder.

"Wait," he said. "I'll bet the kid doesn't have a work permit."

"Shut up, Costas," Manetti said.

His partner stared at him. So did everyone else.

"What did you say?" Costas asked when he finally managed to speak.

"I said shut up. Leave the kid alone. Come on. Let's go find some real criminals for you to snarl at."

Costas shrugged and released me.

Officer Manetti stepped over to Mom and said, "Listen, ma'am, I apologize for the search, but we have to follow up on these things. We have to do our job."

Mom nodded. "I understand."

But as the police left, I wondered how much of the rest of it she'd understand.

35

"Working?" Mom asked. "After everything I've told you? After all the times we've talked about it, you sneak behind my back and get a job?"

"It's not really a job. I'm only there a couple hours a night," I said. "It's not full-time or anything."

"Chad, you've been lying to me." She shook her head and looked away.

I knew what was going through her mind. Dad used to tell her he was working when he wasn't. Now I was doing the opposite. Either way, each of us had lied to her. And I'd just lied again. It wasn't a couple hours. It was three or four.

"At least I'm not a drug dealer," I said. That should be worth something. She could be stuck with a kid like Anthony. Of course, Anthony's mother probably believed her son was an angel.

Mom didn't answer.

"It's my fault, Mrs. Turner," Malcolm said, stepping back into the scene and turning on the charm. "I asked Chad to help out. If you're going to be angry at someone, blame me."

"No," I said, moving between Mom and Malcolm. "Nobody forced me to do anything. I made my own decision. I'll take my own blame."

Malcolm started to speak, but I held up my hand to silence him, then turned toward Mom. "It was my own choice." I wasn't going to hide behind Malcolm. I didn't want him to get me out of trouble by charming Mom or playing some role that would distract her from what I'd done. I was going to take responsibility. I wasn't going to run and duck. Not like my dad. I wasn't going to find someone else to blame.

"Maybe I should let you two talk," Malcolm said.

Mom and I both nodded.

Malcolm looked at me, and then at Mom. "I'm sorry my phone call caused all this trouble. But I'm not sorry I made the call. A very nice girl was about to stumble into a whole lot of danger." He looked back at me as if hoping that I'd understand. "I'd do it again if I had to."

I was really pissed at him for calling the cops. And grateful. Why couldn't anything involving Malcolm ever be simple? Either way, I wasn't about to let him off the hook too easily, so I changed the subject. "Thanks for explaining the money to them," I said. I thought about that day when he hadn't helped me, the day he'd stayed on the bench and let the cops hassle me after Anthony stole the sunglasses. It seemed part of the distant past now. Something that had happened to two other people.

Malcolm grinned, then spoke like a crook from an old gangster movie. "He was wiff me, officer, wiff me da whole time. Honest." He bowed, spun around, and walked out the door.

Mom sat down at the table.

"You can't blame me for the cops coming." I took a seat at the other end.

"That's true."

"But I guess I did stuff you told me not to do." I had to admit my other lie. "Actually, it's not a couple hours. It's more like four. But that's still really just part-time. It's not a full workday or anything."

A trickle of tears ran down her cheeks, making me feel like the rottenest son in the world. She deserved better. She'd grown up so poor and then, at sixteen, been swept away by a guy who'd filled her head with dreams and promises. There'd been nothing but hard work and heart-break. Now I was just adding to the burden. I tried to read all the emotions playing across her face.

"Mom . . . ? Say something."

"It's my fault," she said.

"What?"

"I haven't been here for you. None of this would have happened if I was here."

"Don't blame yourself," I said. "You did what you had to. And you *are* here. You didn't run off somewhere." I thought about all those nights when I could have come home earlier. And the mornings when I'd slept late. Worst of all, I thought about those weeks I'd wasted wrapped in my own misery.

"I've missed so much," she said. "You're growing up."

"Hard to avoid," I said, trying desperately to make her feel better. It wasn't a great joke, but I expected to at least get a smile.

Instead, she shook her head sadly and said, "It's not going to be the two of us much longer."

Oh, man. Those words. I remembered the last time Dad was here. He'd stayed for less than a month. They'd been talking. He must have thought I was asleep. He was getting ready to leave. I heard the door open. *We could have made it, Annie,* he'd said. *We could have made it if it had just been the two of us.*

But it's not just us, she'd told him.

He'd grunted as he picked up his bag. *This wasn't the way we'd planned it.*

It's the way it is, she'd said as the door closed and he walked out of our lives.

That song, "Just the Two of Us"—I hated it.

He'd never wanted me.

But Mom had. She'd let him go. And it had become the two of us—me and Mom. She'd chosen me over him. Now I was growing up. She'd been trying to keep that day from coming. The day when a job, or a girl, or some other inevitable part of life would tear me away from her.

"I'll always be your son," I said. "No matter what I'm doing. No matter where I am." I didn't know what else to say. I didn't know what promises I could keep.

"Do you like the job?" she asked.

I thought about the backbreaking, humiliating, dangerous task of slaving away outside the Bozo tank. "It's not bad. Beats fourteen hours on a roof."

"Just until school starts, right? School's the most important thing."

"Right," I said.

"Promise?"

"I promise." That was one I could keep.

She got up from her chair and hugged me. I hugged her back, holding on to her, trying to store the moment in the vault of memories. Storing it against that time when it would no longer be the two of us.

When we stepped apart, she smiled at me and said, "I'm proud of you, Chad. Very proud. You're not a quitter. That's good."

"Thanks." I glanced at the couch and thought about how close I'd come to quitting everything.

"And Chad?" she said.

"What."

"No more lies. Okay?"

I nodded. "No more lies."

I TRIED TO FIND OUT WHAT HAPPENED TO GWEN. THERE WAS a small story about the raid on page three of the paper the next day, but they didn't list the names of any of the minors. Anthony's brother was mentioned. He'd been arrested for possession, resisting arrest, and allowing underage drinking. The cops had also found a couple unlicensed handguns. Between the guns and the drugs, I could see why they'd been so eager to search my place.

Gwen wasn't at the Cat-a-Pult that evening. I was afraid she'd been arrested. On top of that, I was sure Anthony blamed me for all the trouble. There'd probably be a fight the next time he saw me. But that's not what worried me. What if he'd told Gwen it was my fault? What if she thought I'd made the call? She'd never talk to me again. She'd blame me and hate me.

For all I knew, she was on her way back to Montana. Or juvenile hall.

"Hey," the girl at the Cat-a-Pult called to me. "Try your luck? Come on. You look like a winner."

I shook my head and walked off.

At least there were other parts of my life that weren't hopeless. Jason seemed to be slowly healing. He'd had a couple setbacks, and he was going to need an operation to repair some of the damage to his kidneys, but he was doing better than any of the doctors had expected. They mentioned the possibility of a remission. That's when a disease goes away. Remissions were rare with what Jason had, but they were known to happen. The doctors couldn't explain it. But I could.

I had to work on Malcolm for a couple days before he finally came to the hospital with me. When we got there, he mostly just stood off to the side while I clowned around. Then, when we were getting ready to leave, he found out that Jason liked *Saturday Night Live*. It was almost as if someone had pushed a button. Malcolm started doing these old routines from the early shows, and Jason cracked up. Malcolm could do the voices perfectly. I loved the one where he put the fish in the blender. We stayed so long, I was afraid Jason's mom would catch us. I finally had to drag him away.

"You both coming back tomorrow?" Jason asked as we left.

I looked at Malcolm. He nodded and said, "Hard to pass up a captive audience."

He got that sad look again when we were walking through the corridors past all the rooms full of sick people, but he seemed all right once we got back on the street.

"It's helping," I said as we headed home.

"Yeah, it's helping. If that kid gets any better, we might have to tie him to the bed." He glanced back over his shoulder at the hospital.

"You okay?" I asked.

He nodded. "I'll live."

On our second visit I threw Malcolm a line from a Marx

Brothers movie and he responded right away with the answer. We did the whole routine for Jason. Then he threw me a line from a W. C. Fields routine, and we did that skit. Between the two of us, we kept Jason laughing nonstop.

Malcolm came with me to the hospital pretty often after that. The first time Jason's mom walked in on us while we were clowning around, she exploded.

"Mom," Jason said when he managed to get her attention, "they're my friends. They make me feel better." He sat up in bed to prove his point.

She glared at me, but then Malcolm started talking, explaining how good it was for Jason to laugh. I knew enough to stand aside and let him do that performance as a solo. Some audiences were too tough for me. But not too tough for Malcolm. I could see Jason's mom's eyes soften as Malcolm turned on the charm. By the time he was done, she'd even agreed to read *Anatomy of an Illness*. After that, we didn't have to hide anymore.

A while later I actually caught her smiling at our act, though she pretended not to. I figured it was only a matter of time before she broke down and laughed. Malcolm and I both enjoyed the challenge.

I visited Jason every day. And I continued to study the fine art of being a Bozo. Malcolm taught me other things about acting, too. I even started to understand the hard stuff in some of his acting books.

Finally, in early August, Malcolm told me, "Bob's giving you a tryout tomorrow. Six o'clock. You ready?"

Was I ready to be a Bozo? When I first saw Malcolm in the tank, I thought I could step right in and take his place. I didn't think that now. I realized how tough it was to do a good job.

"You're ready," Malcolm said, answering his own question. He handed me a paper bag. "I got you a present."

I opened the bag and found five tubes of greasepaint and a jar of makeup remover. "Waterproof?" I asked.

"You bet."

I took the greasepaint with me to the hospital the next day. With some help and suggestions from Jason, I worked out my own patented Bozo face. It was pretty cool. I did the usual big red mouth, but instead of stars around the eyes, I made the lids black. And I spiked my hair with gel. Jason said I looked like a punk-goth vampire, but I thought it worked.

I found out that greasepaint was a lot easier to put on than take off. "I wish you could be there," I told Jason as I scrubbed at my face with a wad of tissues.

"Me, too. Don't worry. I'll make it before summer's over."

"Yeah," I said. "You will." I tossed the tissues, gave Jason a light punch on the shoulder, then headed home and killed some time watching movies.

I went to the Bozo tank at five thirty. Malcolm came with me. "Want help?" he asked when I reached the door of the dressing room.

"I'll be fine." I went inside. It was a dingy little hole— just a closet with a stool, a wobbly card table, and a large trash basket. A mirror hung on the wall. A light bulb from a fixture in the low ceiling threw a harsh glare on the room. The table, covered with blobs and stripes of smeared makeup, looked like an abstract painting. I sat on the stool and unscrewed the caps of my greasepaint, trying to ignore the fact that my hands were shaking.

I jumped when the door opened, but it was only Malcolm sticking his head in. "So how do you like show business so far?"

"Great," I answered, but he'd already ducked back out. I started spreading the greasepaint. Despite the practice, I kept messing up. Finally, after redoing parts of it several times, I got my face looking the way I wanted.

"Ready?" I asked myself.

I looked in the mirror and let out a Bozo laugh. Crap, I sounded like a chicken. I tried again and did a bit better.

"Ready now?" I asked my reflection.

I nodded. Ready as I'd ever be. There was no longer any excuse for me to sit there. I slid off the stool and left the room. Outside, I looked around for Mike or Corey. I'd told them about my tryout, but there was no sign of them yet. I hoped they'd show up before I finished.

Waldo, who was working the tank, climbed out when he saw me. "Knock 'em dead, kid," he said, patting me on the back with a wet hand as he passed. "You get stuck, just say, 'Wow. You're ugly.' Works every time. It's my best line, but I don't mind if you use it."

"Thanks."

Malcolm joined me behind the tank. "Just remember one thing."

"What?"

"It's only a stupid boardwalk attraction. It's not life and death. Nothing you do in there will matter tomorrow, so relax and have fun. Don't worry about anything."

"Thanks."

"Oh, one more thing," he said as I opened the gate.

"What?"

"If you mess up, Bob will kill you." He grinned to show me he was kidding. I guess it was his way of getting me to relax. It didn't work.

I climbed into the tank. This was it. Stupid attraction or not, it was a real dunk tank on the best boardwalk in the world, and I was the Bozo. When you run a wheel or a hoop toss, you're just part of the background. Not here. In the tank, the Bozo was the attraction. I could hardly believe I was finally getting my chance. Now I just had to keep from blowing it.

Malcolm stepped over beside Bob and folded his arms against his chest like he was waiting for a show to start. Bob grinned at me, waved with his cotton candy, and said, "Show me what you got."

I scanned the crowd. Wow. There were plenty of people walking past. I realized my problem wouldn't be finding a mark, but narrowing down the choices.

Pick someone.

This was nothing like practicing from the porch. There was a whole mob out there. Hundreds of people were passing by. *Pick someone.*

Who? I spotted a guy with a long beard. What was funny about beards? Maybe I could say there's something hiding in it? No. That wasn't any good. *You look like you're chewing on a chipmunk.* No, too gross. As I struggled to find the perfect line, he cut over to his right and was swallowed by the crowd.

Great. Just wonderful. Here I was, the world's first silent Bozo. Step right up, folks, and dunk the mime.

People flowed past. Some of them glanced at me. But they kept walking. There was no reason for them to stop when there were dozens of more interesting attractions all around. I wasn't interesting. I was mute. Sweat rolled down my forehead from above the edge of the greasepaint. I hadn't even been dunked and my hair was already damp. I looked over at Malcolm.

"You're not Chad," he called. "Stop being Chad."

Yeah. Stop being Chad. I was in a play. A one-man play. Maybe it was called *Lunatic Bozo in a Dunk Tank*. It was a part. Like all the other plays and roles that made up life. *Good Son of a Hardworking Mother. Friend of the Sick Kid. The Errand Boy. The Bad Student.* I had to act. That was all. But I had to make sure that the name of this play wasn't *The Loser.*

Pick someone.

A dorky-looking kid in plaid shorts walked into sight from the left. This was a gift I couldn't refuse. My eyes locked on him like a missile launcher finding a target. "Hey, great shorts!" I shouted as I leaned toward the microphone.

Ouch. Bad move. My amplified voice blasted at me through the speakers. People in the passing crowd flinched.

"Great shorts," I said again, this time speaking at a normal volume that wouldn't rupture any eardrums. "Your mommy know you cut up your couch?" Loud or soft, it was weird to hear myself through the sound system.

Time froze as I waited to see if the mark would take the bait.

A couple people in the crowd laughed. The kid turned toward me. The hook was set. Whoa! It wasn't a nameless mark. It was Corey. Besides the shorts, he was also wearing his extra-nerdy glasses with the thick black frames. I hadn't seen them since he got contacts last year. I smiled as I realized what was going on.

"Where'd you get the glasses from, Dork Vision Center?"

Good old reliable Corey bought a round of balls from Bob and let loose. Knowing him, I figured I was safe and dry for a while. But he managed to nail the target with the third throw. The clang of the ball hitting home caught me by surprise. The lever shot out from the seat and I plunged into the water.

For a moment, all was silence as the water surrounded me. It was eerie, but also beautiful in a way. Here, in the middle of the loudest, craziest place on the planet, I was sheltered from everything. Too bad I didn't have gills so I could stay longer. But I wasn't in the tank to enjoy the peace. I was there to hook the marks. I popped out of the water and put the ledge in place, then crawled back up. I couldn't wipe my face without smearing my makeup, so I jerked my head hard to fling off the drops.

The act of climbing back on the ledge made me feel more like a Bozo. I was into the role now. As I swiveled toward the crowd, I found my next target.

"What are you laughing at?" I said to a woman who was wearing a huge straw hat. She was at the front of a group of five people, and obviously the leader. "Someone just sold you a doormat for your head. You buy *all* your clothes at the hardware store?"

She stepped up to Bob. Out of the corner of my eye, I noticed Mike, wearing his goofiest Hawaiian shirt with pink flamingos and blue parrots on it. I guess he and Corey had decided to give me targets if I needed them. Holy cow—Ellie was there, too, wearing a T-shirt that said, I LOVE TO POLKA, in big red letters. It must have been her dad's. Wow, what great friends. All three were willing to humiliate themselves to help me out. I was a lucky guy. If Jason had been here, he'd have done the same thing. I wondered what—

Whoooooooooooaaa! I was sitting on air as the clang of the struck target echoed in my ears. For a billionth of a second, I hung in space like a cartoon character. Then I dropped like a cartoon anvil. I hit the water hard. The lady had nailed the target while I wasn't paying attention. I let out a shout as I fell. Bad mistake. My mouth filled with water. Oh, lord, I was probably going to need antibiotics. As I stood up, I struggled to smother my coughing. The Bozo doesn't cough. You can't drown a Bozo.

I scampered back up and picked out my next mark. And, as Jason would say, I got into the zone. I developed a rhythm. No doubt, I wasn't as good as Malcolm. I was honest enough to admit that to myself. But I felt I was doing okay, especially for my first time. I hooked a fairly steady stream of vics and lost count of how often I hit the water.

Corey, Mike, and Ellie stayed and watched. Corey had a video camera pointed at the tank. I guess they were making a tape to show Jason. That was cool.

After what seemed like no more than fifteen minutes, Malcolm said something to Bob, who nodded. Then Malcolm walked over to the side of the cage. "Hour's up," he told me.

"So soon? You're kidding?"

He shook his head. "Nope. Time flies when you're getting dunked. But you're handling yourself just fine. Bob and I figure you can keep going until eight if you want."

"Great." I couldn't believe an hour had passed or that they were giving me another. "So I'm doing okay?"

Malcolm nodded. "Yup. But this is no time for chatting. You're letting marks escape."

He stepped aside and motioned for me to get back to work.

I returned my attention to being a Bozo. After a while Malcolm flicked his fingers out three times. I guess he was letting me know I had thirty minutes left. He did it again for twenty.

When he gave me the ten-minute signal, I saw something that stopped me cold right when I was about to hook a new mark. I caught sight of a flash of red weaving through the boardwalk crowd. I followed the motion, remembering the thousand false trails my eyes had chased since the night of the party. But this time it wasn't a mistake. Gwen was walking past.

37

I DIDN'T KNOW WHERE SHE WAS HEADED OR WHAT SHE WAS doing. I just knew there might not be another chance to talk to her. All summer I'd screwed up every opportunity to tell her how I felt. I'd completely blown the simple act of asking her out. Was there any point in trying again?

I realized I had nothing to lose. It's not like she could think any worse of me than she already did.

First I had to keep her from slipping out of reach. "Hey, redhead!" I called. Oh, lord. I clamped my mouth shut as the words shot from the speakers. I was acting like a Bozo chasing a mark—a role I'd been playing for nearly two hours.

Gwen stopped in her tracks and glanced over her shoulder toward the tank. The cry had gotten her attention. My heart froze and my throat closed. She seemed puzzled as she looked at me. I realized she didn't have a clue who the moron was behind the makeup. She didn't know anything about my Bozo dreams. She shrugged and started walking. I couldn't let her go. I had to say something. But I knew it couldn't be an insult, no matter how clever or funny. That would just drive her away. It was time to be myself.

"Gwen," I said, speaking with my own voice. The voice of Chad, not the snarl of the Bozo. "Wait."

She slowed for an instant, but didn't stop.

"Gwen O'Sullivan," I said, so she'd know beyond doubt that I was talking to her. "Don't go."

The crowd stared. My friends stared. They must have wondered what was happening. I didn't care. I'd sought out the dunk tank from the very beginning so I could speak freely. I'd thought I'd only wanted to shout at the world. Now I knew I had other things to say. Quieter things.

I leaned closer to the microphone, desperate for her to hear every word. *Speak the truth,* I thought, as Gwen turned slowly back toward my cage. There was nothing more to lose. "I can't imagine a summer without you," I said, looking straight at her. "Please. Don't walk off. Let me explain."

She took a single step toward the tank.

"Please, Gwen."

She walked past Bob. I slid off the ledge and waded through the water to the front of the cage, clutching the bars for support.

"Chad?" she asked, as if she needed to make sure that the clown who'd just revealed his heart to her was also the boy she knew from the boardwalk.

I nodded. "It wasn't me who called the cops. I didn't want you to go to that party, but I'd never do anything to get you in trouble. Honest. You have to believe me. Just the thought of you there—"

She held up a hand to stop the avalanche of explanations that burst from me. "Chad, I never went inside that house."

"You didn't?"

"I knew Anthony could be kind of wild. But I figured I

could handle things. Like a roller coaster. You know, a safe thrill."

"So why'd you change your mind?"

"When we got there, I could see through the front window what was going on. Beer cans all over. A lot of older guys. You could smell the dope all the way out on the porch." She shook her head. "I sure couldn't handle the stuff that was happening in that place. I didn't even want to try. And I thought about the look in your eyes when I mentioned the party. I got scared. I left as fast as I could."

"I'm glad."

"Me, too." She reached out and put her hand on top of mine where I clenched the bars. Her touch sent a tremor through my body.

"I looked for you," I told her.

"I had to take some time away from everything. My boss understood. I'm off until next week."

I drew a deep breath. I could stay there forever, talking with her, and be happy. But I still hadn't said the things I needed to say the most. "I thought about you every day since we met last year. I couldn't wait to see you again."

An odd smile touched her lips. "Was that so hard to say?" she asked.

"Yeah. No. I don't know. . . ." I realized it was hard—incredibly hard—to say what was in my heart. It had taken me a lifetime to speak those words. But afterward, it was wonderful to know they'd been said.

"I thought about you, too, Chad."

I held on to the moment, feeling the warmth of her hand on mine. Gazing into her eyes. And she gazed back.

I'm not sure which of us was the first to realize how silly

we looked. A wonderfully stunning red-haired girl standing at a dunk tank holding hands with a spike-haired clown who was chest deep in slimy water. But one of us snickered, then the other let out a small laugh, and the next thing I knew we were roaring.

"Sorry," she said when she'd caught her breath. "I wasn't laughing at you."

"Laugh at me," I said. "Laugh with me. Doesn't matter, as long as you keep laughing. Please, don't ever stop laughing."

Another voice entered our world. "I hate to break this up, but maybe you should turn the tank over to someone a bit less goofy," Malcolm said as he joined us. He was already wearing his Bozo face.

"Good idea." Reluctantly I slipped my hand from Gwen's and climbed out of the cage. "Don't go away," I said to her as I headed off to remove my makeup.

"Don't worry, Chad," she said. "I'm not running off with any other clowns."

Jason continued to heal during the rest of the summer. His immune system was under control again, though it would take time for him to recover from all the damage his body had suffered. His doctor took the credit, but Jason and I knew the truth. His mom even started talking to me again. And I finally did get her to laugh, so I guess things healed between us, too. By the end of August, Jason was home and well enough to hang out on the beach. He was off most of the medicine by then and only had to see the doctor every couple weeks. Sick or not, he still had all the girls checking him out when they walked past.

According to Corey, who'd done a lot of research about this particular autoimmune disorder, there were "no known instances of relapse after remission." In plain English, that meant the problem had gone away for good. Jason would have to work hard to get back into condition, but his doctors felt there was no reason he wouldn't be able to play volleyball again by next summer. Knowing Jason, he'd be in excellent shape way ahead of their schedule.

I was in good shape myself. Gwen and I spent nearly all of our free time together, mostly on the beach or on the boardwalk. I never grew tired of being with her. She got along great with Mike and Corey and Ellie. That was no surprise. And with Jason, too, of course. But she didn't look at him the way most girls did. Not even once.

I worked a couple hours as a Bozo almost every day, usually from five to seven, and also chased the balls at the busiest times. Bob paid me for both jobs. I couldn't believe I was making money as a Bozo. The truth is, I would have paid for the chance to be in the tank. Not that I'd ever admit anything like that to Bob.

But no matter what else was going on, I made sure I was home around four on weekdays so I could spend some time with Mom before she headed off to her classes. We threw a small party for her when she got her certificate. Everyone came. Doc was there, and Mom's friends from the diner. The next day she had an interview for a job with a local lawyer. She didn't get it, but she kept looking and two weeks later found a job she liked. She works all day now, but she's home at night—at least until she figures out what class she wants to take next.

Mom's told me more about her and Dad. It wasn't all bad. They'd had some good times. I know she doesn't want me to hate him. I'm trying not to. And I'm trying to accept that I won't turn out like him.

I think Malcolm healed some, too. But at a slower pace. His wounds were a lot deeper than Jason's or mine. I tried to make him laugh whenever I could. I believed it helped.

It was hard to laugh at anything on the day Gwen headed home, but we managed to smile. I knew I'd see her again. In the meantime I had her address and her phone number. I figured I'd be spending a lot of money on phone calls. That was fine with me. I even had her e-mail address. Corey said I could use his computer whenever I needed to. Maybe I'd even get a cheap one for me and Mom.

"Nice girl," Malcolm said when we left the airport. He'd borrowed Doc's car and insisted on driving Gwen and me there so we could have a bit more time together. He even waited in the parking lot while I went inside with her. "Your excellent taste in girlfriends is nicely balanced by her lack of taste in boyfriends."

I nodded and stared out the window at the underside of a jet rising above us.

To Malcolm's credit, he seemed to know that this wasn't the kind of wound that needed to be healed right away. He didn't try to cheer me up. Instead, he made a confession.

"I'm a little nervous about teaching," he said as he merged onto the highway.

"You?"

"Yeah, me."

"It's just another role," I said. "And you've had plenty of practice. If you can teach me, you can teach anyone."

"Speaking of which, I'd like to keep it up, if you don't mind," he said.

"Aren't you ready for a break? The tank's closing for the season anyhow."

"Not that. I want to try my lessons out on you. If you don't mind. Just to see how they work before I do them in class. Okay?"

"You mean you want me to act like a student?" I asked.

"Basically."

"Talk about a rough role. But for you, I'll give it a shot."

"Thanks."

We drove back home and he dropped me off, then went

to return the car to Doc. I wandered around by myself on the beach for a while, then hooked up with Jason. Just as the first night had started with a walk to the end of the boardwalk and back, the last night finished with one.

"Going to be a long school year," I said to Jason. I sighed and slouched down on the bench by the Fifteenth Street ramp, putting my feet up on the rail and watching the ocean turn from blue to gray and then to black as the light faded. Behind us I could hear scattered sounds from the few remaining tourists.

Jason laughed and held out his hand. "Pay up, chump. You mentioned school."

"No mercy?" I asked.

"None."

"Give me a break," I said. "I dragged you from the icy clutches of death."

"And I appreciate it. But you still owe me a dollar."

He owed me one, too, from back when he was in the hospital. But I didn't mention that. Instead, I dug into my pocket and handed him a buck. "Here. Put it in the California fund."

"I thought you didn't want to go there."

"Who knows?" I said. "It might be a good place to spend some time."

"Think so?" Jason asked.

"Yeah. Be kind of weird, though. Watching the sun set into the ocean. Seems kind of unnatural."

"Yeah, like putting cheese on the bottom of a burger. I suppose I could get used to it," Jason said. "You really think you'd go?"

"Yeah. I think I might." I thought about the world beyond the boardwalk. Malcolm had given me a taste for acting. Santa Monica was close to Hollywood, which was a good place to be if you wanted to work as an actor. Not that I was sure I was crazy enough to try something like that. I smiled as I thought how Mom would react. She wouldn't be thrilled about me making that kind of career choice. On the other hand, she'd let me work as a Bozo, so anything was possible.

And everything was possible.

I saw that now. You didn't have to live the rest of your life with your first choice. A choice isn't a tattoo. You can try things out, test the waters. Santa Monica didn't have to be forever.

A sense of peace settled over me as I watched the surf creep higher with the rising tide. Life wasn't a passing mark you had to hook or lose forever. I had time.

Maybe Mom could get a job out there. Maybe Gwen would go to college somewhere not too far away. Maybe I'd even go to college. Become a doctor or a lawyer. Or a scientist. Or maybe even a professor of dunkology.

Don't laugh. Stranger things have happened.

ACKNOWLEDGMENTS

It's time for some thank-you notes.

This book had a long, strange odyssey from idea to reality, and there are many people who helped. During one of the lean years, Marilyn and Richard Gomes generously allowed my family to spend a week in their condo at the Jersey shore. It was there, on a board-walk, that *Dunk* was born. Even then I had help. I tell people I'm the world's least-observant writer. It was my wife, Joelle, who pointed to a particularly sinister Bozo and said, "He's just like a character from one of your stories." I'd recently published a collection that featured various dark and hungry creatures, carnival monsters, strange road-side attractions, and other horrors. She was right. The Bozo was compelling. When I got home, I wrote a chapter about a boy who is mesmerized by such a performance. I even volunteered to take a turn in a dunk tank at a local school carnival, just for the experience.

The chapter sat for years. I wrote other books, mostly fantasy. But I started writing some realistic short stories, too. Those stories inspired me to try a major novel set fully in the real world. The dor-mant chapter called to me. As I wrote, I felt the unease that comes from exploring new territory. No monsters in this book. No wizards or vampires. At times I was excited. At other times I was positive I was creating hundreds of pages of rubbish. Deep in my heart, I nour-ished the faint hope that I was writing something special.

Like any highly insecure writer, I sought feedback. Various peo-

247

ple were kind enough to read the chapters that I thrust at them. Brian Macdonald was one of the first. Marilyn Singer and the ever-reliable Doug Baldwin each read an early draft and provided many excellent suggestions. Doug's daughters, Fern and Heather, and his wife, Connie Cook, are also members of my all-star critique squad. Carolyn and Ashley Grayson read various drafts. Dian Curtis Regan provided all sorts of feedback. My daughter, Alison, served as critic-on-demand, sounding board, and brainstorming resource. My wife, who probably regrets ever pointing out that first Bozo, was handed the thankless role of constant reader.

An extremely patient Dr. Matthew S. Pollock, whom I shamelessly cornered in the waiting area of a karate dojo while we watched our kids punch each other, answered dozens of questions about various medical aspects of the book. To his credit he never ran or flinched when I waved pages in his face. Any errors in this area are mine, not his.

Alick Smith III served as my roofing expert. Any leaks are mine, not his.

Once the easy task of writing was out of the way, I faced the hard part: finding an editor. It was Marilyn Singer who suggested Michele Coppola and provided an introduction. Nobody has ever done me a greater favor. Shelly is a dream editor. Her gentle suggestions helped the book grow in many ways. I give heartfelt thanks to her, and to everyone at Clarion, for sharing my enthusiasm. I need to give special thanks to managing editor James Armstrong for lending an ear and an eye that are far more skilled than my own. He caught every ball I dropped.

Anatomy of an Illness is a real book. We all owe a debt of thanks to the late Norman Cousins for sharing his insights. The boardwalk where Chad lives is loosely based on the one I visited. My thanks to the barkers, Bozos, pitchmen, merchants, cooks, waiters, policemen, lifeguards, and visitors who make it so special. Any seedy or unpleasant aspects are entirely my own invention. I love every inch of that place.

Finally, thanks to Doc Watson and J. S. Bach for creating such wonderful music. Their artistry is as much a part of my workday as my cats, coffee cup, and computer.

I could go on. There's nothing easier for writers than to write about their books. But I've already overstayed my welcome. Visit me at my website (www.davidlubar.com) if you have a chance. I can promise you a few laughs.

DAVID LUBAR grew up in New Jersey and now lives next door in Pennsylvania. Armed with a degree in philosophy from Rutgers University and no marketable job skills, he spent several years as a starving writer before accidentally discovering he knew how to program computers. He is now a full-time writer and the author of eleven books for teens and young readers, including the fantasy *Hidden Talents*. He lives with his wife, daughter, and three cats.